I0685816

UNRESOLVED

...a question of leadership

Philip St Lawrence

Clink Street

London | New York

Published by Clink Street Publishing 2019

Copyright © 2019

First edition.

The author asserts the moral right under the Copyright, Designs and
Patents Act 1988 to be identified as the author of this work.

Historical and contemporary fiction. Central characters set in 2018 are
imaginary and any resemblance to real persons is entirely coincidental.

ISBN:
978-1-912850-52-5 paperback
978-1-912850-53-2 ebook

Dedicated to my family
Loved beyond measure – in celebration of our nation's finest
moments, suspended for now but to be restored at a later date

Introduction

It is 2018 and Great Britain is witnessing one of the most dramatic political dramas in recent history playing out with monumental consequences for the future. At the epicentre in Whitehall, Maggie Taylor wrestles with her responsibilities in negotiating her country's exit from the European Union. Whilst doing so she reads the unfolding story of Alfred the Great in bringing freedom for his people, which we follow in tandem with her.

How strange it is this novel reaches its climax upon Remembrance Day, the day we recall the more recent sacrifices for freedom; the very day too I put down my pen having completed the work. Strange also that the date of publication happens to be within days of what some are calling 'Independence' Day. Strange too this is also the anniversary of Alfred's darkest moment when he finally reached his hiding place at Athelney in 878.

It is reputed that a commentator once declared to Sir Winston Churchill that he was the greatest Englishman. Churchill instantly corrected him. That soubriquet belonged to Alfred he told him. Certainly in Churchill's 'History of the English-Speaking Peoples' he is effusive about the medieval king, Britain's only king ever to be conferred the epithet 'the Great'.

1

We are fortunate indeed that thanks to the Anglo-Saxon Chronicle and the biography written by Bishop Asser in 893, we have precise information about his life. I openly admit to some indulgences but this is intended only to depict the scene and bring his glorious darkest hour alive for the reader. It is then no surprise that to the inquisitive mind of Maggie Taylor she finds inspiration from her hero as well as from Churchill himself.

There are similarities too between her and Alfred: her high moral code and beliefs, her unashamed patriotism and respect for the people and her intrepid resolve to see Britain's negotiation through no matter what the sacrifice. Her own darkest hour beckons as her story unfolds.

Chapter 1

December 877

It was a damp December dawn. Christmas of 877 was still two weeks away and the temperature had dropped in the last couple of days. Alfred shivered uncontrollably even though the embers of the fire still gave off signs of life. Around him the little settlement at Chippenham was slowly coming to life. The noise of movement could be heard outside. He looked up through the dank dark mist trying to focus his eyes. Sleep had evaded him but it was not just the cold that had kept him awake.

His mind was racing as it had done many times since his retreat from Wareham. He had asked himself a hundred times whether he had been right to negotiate a truce with Guthrum a year ago: the occupation of Wareham had been truly horrific for its inhabitants. The Viking leader had exacted a high price both in silver and in hostages as he had agreed to leave Exeter as well as Wareham and for the moment anyway, Wessex. But should Alfred have not fought and made his stand at Wareham when he had had the chance? Had he not been naive to have trusted Guthrum to keep to the deal they had negotiated? After all, Guthrum had not kept his word. In a sense he had made a mockery of

3

Alfred as he had moved on to Exeter in defiance of his oath, before finally retreating.

Ealswith has tried to console him. She had exhorted him to believe he had acted wisely, in the only way he could. Not only had Alfred saved himself from a probable defeat, he had saved his army to fight another day she had insisted. But then Ellie, as Alfred called her affectionately, loved Alfred more than she could say. From that day nine years earlier when they had married after Alfred had come to their aid in Mercia, she had indeed felt devoted to him. She knew not what it was that attracted her. His looks perhaps, his intelligence for sure. Their relationship had blossomed and evolved: gradually, just gradually she had come to realise that she had married a king with aspirations for his people and a determination somehow to turn those dreams into reality. For sure Alfred was no ordinary Anglo-Saxon warrior, and she knew it and had allowed it to excite her. Now as she lay beside him as dawn broke, she suddenly became aware of footsteps.

"Sire, I need to speak to you." Ellie looked up. She recognised the scarred face that peered through their damp enclosure. It made her wince though she had seen that face many times.

Alfred sat up slowly and gazed at their intruder. "What is it Edgar?" he asked.

"Sire, we have caught three more spies passing as traders. We persuaded them to talk". He allowed a grin to emanate from his grisly features as he said the words. Ellie knew his meaning.

"The Vikings are still at Gloucester but more, many more are coming." He sounded agitated, gesturing feverishly.

"Calm yourself my friend, tell me precisely what you

4

know," Alfred demanded. He stood intent upon discerning the new intelligence.

"Messengers were sent by Guthrum to Ubba in Dublin asking him to come. He is bringing ships and men to join the Great Army at Gloucester. Should we not depart Chippenham Sire before they attack – or else part with more silver?"

For a moment Alfred said nothing. He looked first to Ellie then back to Edgar. He knew that after the retreat from Wareham his magnates had lost a little of their faith in him. These men, powerful land owners as they were, had become anxious; they had heard of the fate of their counterparts in the kingdoms of Mercia and East Anglia under their new overlords. The Viking tide seemed to them inexorable and too often their response had been to buy their peace. But Alfred now rejected their willingness to concede endlessly. He had determined he would have no truck with it. He spoke calmly, his tone unruffled by the news.

"You have done well to tell me of this. But you want me to succumb again; to pay them off but let me be plain with you. We will only negotiate. We will never donate to them what is not theirs. Have we not learned at Wareham and at Exeter that when we give more they simply demand more? Have we learned nothing? We will turn this around. Trust me Edgar; do not lose your nerve."

For a few seconds neither man spoke. It was Edgar who broke the silence.

"Sire, Guthrum is tempting the magnates and aldermen. He has told them they will be saved and allowed to keep their lands if they will change their allegiance. Guthrum will do anything now to take Wessex from under you."

5

Instantly Alfred raised himself to his full height. His voice came more strongly. "Little do you understand me. Know this and tell it to the aldermen. I do not stand only for the establishment, for the wealthy landowners. I stand for the people, all the people. We will remain in Chippenham till Christmas has passed and then we shall prepare ourselves for what will follow. We will not show weakness now, just resolve Edgar, just resolve, is that understood my friend?"

Edgar said nothing. He gazed expressionless at his sovereign. A silence followed between the two men which neither broke. Then Edgar bowed his head and made to leave. As he did so, Alfred called after him causing him to pause and turn.

"One thing more. I will not project fear to my people to frighten them into compromise. It is a positive vision that will make us strong, that and determination. Be sure of that and stand with me Edgar, I beseech you."

Summer 2018

Maggie Taylor put the book down intrigued at what she had read. When she was not grappling with the Brexit negotiations her favourite hobby was reading history, especially early English history. Alfred she had mused held a particular attraction for her, perhaps more so than Arthur and her other heroes she had studied. For a start unlike Arthur, Alfred's fascinating life had been recorded by the Saxon Chroniclers and for the most part could be relied upon. No doubt the writer had embellished Alfred's story around the facts but for Maggie it had helped to depict what it must have been like all those years ago.

Moreover the pressures she was under as she tried her best to facilitate the ever changing minds and vicissitudes of her political masters necessitated some relief and aside from her love of classical music, studying history relieved her of her stress.

Now two years after the historic referendum result, aged just 33 she had found herself seconded as a high flying civil servant into the Downing Street team negotiating Britain's independence from the EU. The term independence though was not one that was ever used in her circle of power. Accommodation would have been a preferred description. On the coffee table in front of her in her smartly decorated lounge were strewn an array of papers, all of which were marked confidential and all of which would have been dynamite she knew to those supporting Brexit. Yet she was devoutly observant to maintaining her strict protocols and to conforming to her establishment colleagues. She had not gained a double first at Cambridge without being astute and Maggie was astute enough to realise that to fail to follow the line laid down by her political masters would be a bad career move.

Today was Saturday however and she knew she could afford a few hours to switch off and engage her restless mind upon other things – things like Alfred. However, she had done enough reading for the moment. She stood and stretched and looked around. Her flat in Kensington Church Street looked nice she thought, not flashy but simply nice and that was how she liked it. She had contemplated a new picture above the fireplace she had spotted at a

Knightsbridge gallery: it was expensive but she could afford it, though Maggie never spent money frivolously. Her father had brought her up to respect money as an investment tool and those values had remained with her. She walked to the window and took in the view. Outside, afternoon strollers and busy shoppers were out in abundance. The last throes of the hot summer sunshine of 2018 had been almost too much. She threw open the windows hoping for some respite.

It was then she spotted the red Porsche parking oppo- site. She waved as her current lover, Onslow Ratcliffe looked up and saw her. She knew she was on the rebound after not marrying the man to whom she had been devoted. She knew too that Ratcliffe was unlike her in so many ways: a snob to put it bluntly, smug and arrogant in equal measure and yet in some strange way she could forgive him for that. He was after all handsome, intelligent and generous towards her. For the moment anyway that was what she craved.

As she waited for him she glanced at the mirror and checked her hair. She looked just fine she thought. She had dressed casu- ally but tastefully as she always did. Her thick brown hair had a lustre about it that men seemed to find attractive, framing her pretty face which exhibited a certain intellectual air. In that department she was certainly the match of most of her admir- ers of whom there were plenty. But Maggie had never been vain about her looks. Indeed she rather took a dislike to those who were inordinately narcissistic. Men could take her as they found her as far as she was concerned. Besides, it was the person underneath that ought to matter she had told herself.

Minutes later she embraced Ratcliffe and placed a glass of cold Sauvignon Blanc in his hand. They touched glasses. She looked him up and down. Four years older than her, he stood

8

a little over six feet tall, too good looking by half somehow commensurate with his rakish charm. But she liked what she saw. He dressed well though perhaps a little dapper for her taste. She couldn't resist feeling attracted to him, his blue eyes with just a hint of the rotter about him that affirmed his overly large ego and sense of importance; characteristics that for now she could forgive him for.

After a while they stepped out arm in arm and sauntered in the direction of Holland Park. She had always loved the place, combining as she saw it a peculiar tranquility and elegance; an attractive relief to the endless commotion of London life. When they returned, she opened the fridge and poured them each another glass of cold wine. The taste felt good against her palate and when they simultaneously put their glasses down she felt the need to kiss Ratcliffe passionately. He reciprocated, his hands passing up her body finding their way slowly, lightly, to caress her breasts. She began to moan softly in his ear. Moments later Maggie led him by the hand into her bedroom and they made love.

It was the next day on a leisurely Sunday morning that she picked up the book she had been so assiduously reading. She opened it feeling a curious need to talk to Onslow about the issues it raised. For as she had begun to steel her way into the character and actions of Alfred, she couldn't help but discern an intellectual correlation to her challenges at work. Whilst Maggie herself had studiously maintained a neutral stance she had become aware that Ratcliffe might be allowing his Remainer sympathies to colour his work. To share her inner thoughts with him would be nice, stimulating even, though his response she instinctively knew might not be receptive. She would test the water tentatively she determined.

"Onslow," she asked, "you told me you studied classics at Oxford. Tell me, do you have an interest in history, in Alfred the Great for instance?"

Onslow Ratcliffe stood in the middle of the room dressed in blue chinos and a matching open shirt. He looked at her surprised by her question.

"I know next to nothing about Alfred except that he burned the cakes that is! Why do you ask Maggie?"

Her mind raced back to Alfred's stern response to Edgar; to his insistence upon not conceding endlessly to the Vikings; to his determination to inject positivity not fear to move his people; to his affirmation of representing the people rather than the landowning establishment. She began slowly at first to share with him what she had read. At first Ratcliffe listened. At first she held his attention but then as he sensed what she was getting at his response changed. She persisted however, eager to share her thoughts.

"Alfred learnt that giving concessions to the Vikings gave him only temporary relief. He learnt that being too generous simply encouraged them to go for more. Are we not guilty of that Onslow? Are we and our political masters not conceding too much and getting far too little back in exchange?" she asked. Her mind flashed to their negotiation discussions due to resume in Whitehall the next day; to the steady evisceration of the Brexit project she had witnessed.

"Everybody knows we have to do that to keep the status quo. We need to change as little as possible," Onslow retorted.

"But what sort of a negotiation is that? We've offered £39 billion – and we both know it will be twice that eventually, but for what? For the privilege of allowing the EU to sell more to us than we do to them," she went on. "Are we not giving away too much Onslow, really, so much in exchange for so little?"

Her rhetorical question just for a moment silenced him. He stared out of the window conjuring up his response. As he spoke he kept his back to her.

"We have to Maggie. We have to keep the status quo to keep the economy on the road. As I said, we need to change things as little as possible and that's precisely what we're doing."

Maggie breathed in deeply.

"On whose say so?" she interrupted him. "On whose say so? Only the establishment. But Onslow there are plenty of economists and experts who believe we can be better off independent. The IMF and Brussels have, as you know very well, confirmed that 90% of world economic growth over the coming 15 years will come from outside the EU. Every year the EU share of world trade drops even more. Alfred didn't settle for compromise permanently with the Vikings. He promised to the people something very different Onslow – freedom!"

Maggie in some strange way now felt moved by her own rhetoric. She had always relished a vigorous debate. To have one with the smug but clever Onslow Ratcliffe did not intimidate her in the slightest. It was then he turned to face her.

"Maggie, our best bet is to stay close to Europe. Forget about independence and freedom. In the modern world that is not what is important. We must stick with the status quo," he repeated.

"On whose say so Onslow, on whose say so? The establishment, the CBI, the BBC, the House of Lords, the institutions who are kept comfortable? These are the same institutions

11

Onslow who were wrong about the exchange rate mechanism, wrong about prices and incomes in Heath's day, wrong about the Thatcher reforms, wrong about the Euro! What about the people Onslow? What about the people?" she persisted. She felt her hackles rise still further.

"What do the people know?" Ratcliffe retorted. "What do the people know? Most are ignorant and uneducated!" he exploded.

Maggie couldn't believe what she was hearing now. Yes, she had heard similarly arrogant views from others – but not from Onslow, not until this moment. It did nothing to endear him to her. She stood closer now her tone rising with her anger.

"Tell that to the people of Poland since the war. Tell it to the Estonians, Onslow. Tell it to the Ukrainians, tell it to those whose loved ones have died for their freedom," she persisted. Now it was Maggie with invective in her voice. She was in no mood to give in to him. "Of course freedom is still important. Your grandfather fought for it and my grandfather fought for it and millions of others too! We had a referendum Onslow. It's called democracy!"

Onslow Ratcliffe did not respond. He stood stupefied by this blistering onslaught, staring out of the window but seeing nothing. His mind was swirling but if he continued he knew he was in danger of destroying his relationship with Maggie. He had already fallen out with friends over his Brexit views, but to fall out with Maggie was a step too far. As if reading his thoughts Maggie paused. She also had no wish to increase the tension between them still further.

She stood in front of him and took his hands in hers. She squeezed them gently and smiled: it was not a smile of submission however, far from it. She looked deep into his eyes trying to read his innermost thoughts. Would it be possible to find some agreement she wondered? In a sense it resembled their negotiations with Brussels. When bottom lines failed to overlap, she knew only too well there could be no win-win outcome; only defeat for one party or a no deal conclusion.

Maggie Taylor had been tutored upon negotiation skills before she had been transferred from the Brexit Department to Downing Street. During the weeks of intensive discussions with Brussels, she had witnessed at first hand a generosity with concessions, often not made conditional but given in a futile effort to move the negotiation along. It had worked but at enormous cost. They had broken many of the laws of negotiation but she had been powerless to stop it. The conciliation so aptly illustrated by Onslow's attitude had become unrelenting. Nevertheless she had determined to stick to her supportive brief as the assiduous civil servant that she was.

Outside, the noise of sirens as an emergency vehicle passed now broke the silence between them. But it was only a temporary respite.

"I'm sorry Maggie. I had no wish to get angry. Let's not fall out over this." Onslow's tone had changed. Gone was the hint of superiority and in its place just a hint of humility. He saw Maggie's eyes look down as if she were playing her next words over in her mind.

"Onslow, I will say only this." She spoke slowly with calm conviction, never taking her eyes off his. "We are not giving the people what they voted for. They resent 70% of our laws being made by unelected, unaccountable foreigners. We are selling Brexit in name only, Brino, to the people and my bet is

13

they are seeing through it. We are deceiving our own people, Onslow. The Brexit vision I truly believe does not exist in Downing Street and we are conspirators in the game. That vision is being denied them because it doesn't truly exist."

Onslow Ratcliffe remained expressionless. If he agreed even remotely with this assertion he was not going to show it. Only when later he left did Maggie resume her reading. The question of what Alfred would do next intrigued her.

Chapter 2

January 878

As the little settlement of Chippenham had celebrated Christmas Day in 877, thoughts of the Vikings being just 29 miles away in their fortified location at Gloucester had been just for the moment held in abeyance. Alfred had refused to allow a sense of defeatism to take hold. However, with the Great Heathen Army of Guthrum holding the western part of Mercia, he was keenly aware the Vikings were within three days march.

Unlike the Anglo-Saxon kingdoms of Northumbria, Mercia and East Anglia he had managed somehow to keep Wessex, stretching from Cornwall in the west to Thanet in the east and everything south of the Thames, at least to a degree free of the Vikings. Admittedly the list of towns that had been plundered and sometimes occupied by the heathen hordes was substantial: Winchester, London, Salisbury, Thanet, Reading, Wareham, Exeter, Wallingford and Basingstoke had all been fought over. Yet through a mixture of victories, calculated retreats and negotiated deals, Alfred had cleverly evaded capture. He had proved himself an inspirational commander, marshalling the sparse resources offered by the Wessex fyrd and willing to take the fight to the enemy.

But now Christmas had come and gone. The early days of January were already upon them and Alfred was restless. Something was worrying him; something he couldn't put his finger on, but which needled him and made him anxious. He felt a curious sensation that all was not right. The New Year had arrived bringing with it a peculiar and somewhat worrying sense of anticipation in the air. In the room reserved in its simple format for Ellie and himself, he sat amidst an array of rugs strewn over the straw floor offering some semblance of luxury as befitted the king. For the season it was not cold. Nevertheless a small fire flickered, crackling as at regular intervals he threw wood upon it that had retained its moisture. It was a pleasing sound though: a sound that told of home, of peace, of comfort.

He sat quite still staring into the flames steadying his mind as visions of the Vikings so near filled his thoughts. Earlier in the day he had been able to relax. With chosen friends, armed in case of coming across Viking raiders, he had spent a couple of hours hunting. They had ridden south of Chippenham passing little homesteads dotted here and there. The sun had shone bringing relief to the dampness that had prevailed over Christmas. The great grassy meadows interspersed with varied forest fauna had resumed their splendour and the fresh breeze had felt good on his face as he had ridden hard.

He looked up suddenly finding his thoughts interrupted. Ellie had entered. She looked beautiful he thought in the evening light. The flickering flames seemed to pick out her features casting a radiant sensual glow over her skin. A blue coloured garment was loosely draped over her shoulders over which Ellie's fair hair hung loosely but provocatively.

Alfred reached up and took hold of her hand: he pulled her gently down beside him in front of the crackling fire. They said nothing to each other but the chemistry between them was palpable.

She reached over and poured water into a goblet and put it to his lips before sipping from it herself. Still she said nothing, instead letting her lips touch his. She let them linger lightly, feeling the sensation of his wet lips on hers. Neither pulled away, each content to savour the moment. His hand now cupped hers. His fingers stroked her skin sending pulses of pleasure running through her body. Ellie drew her face back and smiled at him waiting for Alfred's response.

He kissed her gently, lovingly. His hand moved to her shoulder stroking it as if she were a painting of priceless quality before sliding provocatively down her body. Still neither spoke, neither wishing to break the magical spell. But each knew what they desired. Their love, unquestioned between them needed again to be satiated. To many men their women were little more than chattels and their love-making was little more than the lustful satisfying of carnal pleasure. But Alfred's love for Ellie was genuine and caring. Her pleasure was as important if not more important than his own. He turned towards her and lifted the garment slowly over Ellie's shoulders before lowering her on to the rug. Then he leaned over her. He brushed his lips across her neck tantalisingly, content to linger, playing with Ellie, leaving her begging silently still for him to kiss her breasts. Her back arched; suddenly she felt those lips move to where she wanted them, the sensations almost too much to bear.

She revelled in his tenderness, every sensation of intimacy squeezed through her very being, its manifest love destined for her Ellie, and her alone. Her eyes had closed as she had submitted to her lover, yet submission was hardly the word: she had freely given herself to him; she had relished and adored this man for nine years and this moment of intimacy was just one of many.

But their need to make love, to couple their bodies as one, could no longer be frozen in time, denied and held in eternal suspense. They moved slowly at first, together in perfect unison. Alfred, this Alfred, the courageous warrior able to slash and parry with the enemy, to use his innate strength to destroy his enemies, to match violence with violence – this same Alfred with the greatest tenderness now lay in her arms, the lover who satisfied her beyond measure.

The exquisiteness of her pleasure was overwhelming for Ellie as the end came. Throughout neither had spoken. Only her moans had broken the stillness of the air as she had writhed in his arms whimpering her cries of pleasure. But finally words came. It was Alfred who spoke first.

"I love you," he whispered into her ear. Then he blew into it a kiss. She giggled. She looked deep into his eyes. "I love you too," she declared.

For a long while they lay with their arms entwined. The evening had turned into night and in only an hour it would be the 6th January, the feast of Epiphany and the twelfth night after Christmas. Celebrations had been planned marking the coming of the Magi to the infant Jesus but for now the little Chippenham settlement containing the royal household at its centre slept silently. But sleep evaded Alfred. His mind was restless. Sensing him immersed, lost in thought Ellie kissed him and then spoke.

"My darling you can't sleep. What is it?"

He hesitated. "I don't know," he said softly. He held her close and gazed into her eyes as he continued, speaking slowly as the words came to him. "I have so many dreams for my people Ellie, so much that needs to be done."

She looked at him inquisitively. "Talk to me Alfred. Tell me your thoughts, tell me your dreams."

She kissed him tenderly, encouraging him to share what was on his mind. For a moment he said nothing as he wrestled to turn the thoughts into coherent language.

"We are facing an enemy Ellie which wants to destroy our liberty and shackle us to their ways."

He paused as if giving time for her to assimilate the significance of his words. "The witan, the people – my people, they want to be free. They want us to be in control of our own laws." Alfred hesitated. He had no wish to bore Ellie. He was well aware she was her own woman, intelligent and with her own views upon the Viking menace. Yet he knew also Ellie had stood by him, not as a dutiful wife but because she cared about their relationship and genuinely shared many of his beliefs.

"I am going somehow to give my people their independence, free of being under foreign rule," he continued. "That is my vision!"

He paused again not taking his eyes off hers, seeking some indication of her assent.

"I will not concede anymore," he continued. "We won't live under a system of vassalage like our brothers in Mercia. We deserve more. Our people deserve more."

Ellie thought for a moment and then responded.

"Your father Ethelwulf had the same vision didn't he?" She squeezed his arm and cuddled up to his body as he opened up to her.

"He was a fine man. He fought the Vikings just as I do." The story his father had told him of his stand at Charmouth flashed through his mind.

"He had that vision and he passed it on to me. The battle must go on Ellie until it is won – and won it will be!" He sat up taking both of her hands in his and looked intently at her.

"It does not stop there though. To win that freedom we need to refine the burh system with local fortifications just twenty miles apart: a local militia which will be mounted and come together the instant the Vikings threaten."

Ellie nodded. She clasped him to her as she took in his words. Alfred's mind was now swirling. For some reason the need to unload his vision to her was overwhelming.

"There is more," he continued. His tone now changed as he continued to expound his goals to her. Now he spoke more animatedly, gesturing to her in his enthusiasm.

"I want ships that are bigger than those of the Vikings, perhaps 60 oars or more so we can defend our island home before they land on our shores. And something else too – I will bring teaching to my people Ellie, perhaps translating the book of Psalms so they become learned."

He paused again. But Ellie was listening intently being careful not to break this outpouring.

"And I will administer laws so that disputes will be settled through the power of courts. I want evil men to be held to account ..."

Ellie put her hand on his mouth stopping him suddenly. She was not shocked. She had heard Alfred speak this way before. Instinctively she knew it was more than simply a dream and she was happy to stand by her man. She stroked her finger over the palm of his hand and kissed him gently.

"Alfred my love, I will support you no matter what we go through: the witan and the people will share your vision too because you are a leader and you inspire them. It will come to pass my love, I know it will."

For the moment she had reassured him just as she had on numerous occasions before. Alfred was still young and strong but she knew of his vulnerabilities; of his loneliness as the king of Wessex and the pressures upon him. If he lost his nerve in the face of the Viking menace then her perceptive mind was all too aware of the consequences for his kingdom. If he was to have any chance of seeing his dreams become a reality he needed her support and if being a rock was in some way dutiful then she didn't see it that way. She would remain as resolute in her support to her dear Alfred as at any time during their long ordeal.

However there was another aspect to Alfred's vulnerability that could debilitate him with its pernicious bouts of stomach pain. Since the day of their marriage Ellie had been aware of the illness that afflicted him when it struck out of the blue, without warning as if challenging him to defeat it. Alfred did his best to mask it from her but she knew the pain at times was hard to bear. At least for now as they lay in each other's arms the discomfort had left him.

They clasped each other tightly and for several minutes only the silence of the night could be heard in the royal household.

Then, quite suddenly without warning a terrible commotion could be heard outside. The fearsome thunder of horsemen galloping into the settlement shattered the peace in the darkness. Alfred sat up with a start. Instantly he felt his heart thumping. He wrenched at Ellie pulling her up quickly. He raced outside grabbing his sword as he ran. A dozen men had dismounted from horses and were advancing towards the royal household. Alfred shouted to his sentries and amidst the commotion more men rushed to shield their king from the intruders.

But the horsemen were shouting aloud for Alfred. When they recognised him in the darkness they stopped smartly and bowed their heads.

"Sire, stir yourself at once. There is no time to spare," came a shout. Alfred recognised the voice. It was Edgar who had been on patrol keeping tabs on the Viking movements.

"Sire, the Great Heathen Army is on the move. They have left Gloucester and there is not a moment to spare." There was fear in the man's voice, a desperate awful fear.

"Where did you come across them Edgar? Where do you believe them to be now?" Alfred demanded.

"They came by surprise to Cirencester after dusk. We have ridden hard to give you warning. They have already reached the Fosse Way. They will be here by dawn to be sure."

Ellie had followed Alfred outside. She gave a gasp as she took in the news. She clung to his arm, for a moment phased, unable to think clearly. She looked up at the man she loved.

Alfred knew full well what needed to happen now. He had prepared for this moment though had not expected Guthrum to move so soon. Once again the Viking leader had struck with devastating surprise. Alfred's forces were depleted. As so often before, he had determined he would only take them on in battle if he calculated he could win.

Somehow he had to stay alive. He had to withdraw and wait until he had gathered forces sufficient in strength to defy Guthrum. If he attempted to hold out here in

Chippenham and was defeated, all Wessex would fall to the Viking hordes. For Guthrum was desperate to depose him; to put his own lackey in charge of this, the final kingdom to hold out against the Viking onslaught. He had to be stopped.

"Edgar, give orders that we will make haste to depart now. We must stay together and make our retreat to the south. All men wishing to flee with their women and children are free to do so. But they must depart now and may God go with them. All should take whatever provisions they can carry."

Ellie stared at Alfred as he issued his orders. His tone was uncompromising, strangely unnerved and with a suggestion of reassurance to those around him.

"We must empty Chippenham under cover of darkness or else pay the price. Run each of you," Alfred commanded his horsemen. "Run between the dwellings and give these orders. Everything depends upon your speed. Run, I tell you!"

Within minutes the sleeping occupants of tiny humble dwellings were roused from their slumbers. Motivated by fear, the impulse to run was suddenly overwhelming. The gaiety of Christmas and celebrations of the Epiphany were immediately, irrevocably cast aside. In the darkness of that January night men, their adrenaline driving them on, now shepherded their frightened women and children from their homes, some in carts but many more on foot. Where they headed for, they knew not, other than the need to travel south or west to Wales, and get as far away as possible.

Alfred with his depleted retinue and his dearest Ellie now loaded their horses at lightning speed and raced out of Chippenham also. Somehow, through guile and guts, through speed and quick thinking, he had to elude Guthrum once again. If he were to fail, then Alfred knew all that he cared for, all hopes for his people, all hopes for liberty for his country, all would be dashed. The very existence of the free kingdom of Wessex – the cornerstone for all the dreams he had spelt out to Ellie, the base from which freedom for all England could be exacted – depended upon their success in evading capture.

This was indeed the country's darkest hour.

Summer 2018

Maggie Taylor looked up from her book and stared out of the window. She watched as the flat dry farmland flashed by: identical fields save for the varying shades of green and brown as sunlight and shade fought for supremacy through white cirrus clouds. The Eurostar had been late leaving Brussels but she was too tired to care. She would make her cosy little flat in Kensington that evening and that was all that mattered. Besides, her book on Alfred had kept her interest and admiration as she had read. For sure the writer had employed a degree of poetic licence but she knew the Saxon Chroniclers had set out the pertinent facts with an attention to detail.

Her mind flickered between the vision Alfred had so clearly set his heart upon and the situation in which she now found herself immersed. Where was the vision from her political masters she wondered? What would Britain look like after Brexit? Where was the vision of a low tax thriving economy eager to capitalise upon global trade opportunities? Where was the talk of pop concerts and parties to celebrate the nation returned to its sovereign destiny? Instead Downing Street had simply managed the process in true technocratic fashion engaging with one problem after another with never any vision of the broad sunlit uplands to come. How depressing it all felt. A dose of Alfred's inspirational leadership was surely badly needed.

The fields had changed their shade again. Below her immaculate rows of Portland stone headstones signalled another of the British war cemeteries. She thought of the hundreds of thousands of British manhood who had died terrible deaths in northern Belgium. She thought of the trenches. She thought of the sacrifice during the finest hundred days in the history of the British army when these lands had been granted again their liberty. She thought of WW2. She thought of Wellington defending Brussels against Napoleon. How ironic it was that her negotiating British side had been treated with little more than contempt today in that very city.

As she ruminated on the day's negotiation she was not in a happy mood. Time and again she had witnessed her colleagues conceding details that should have been exchanged and made conditional. It depressed her more than she could say but once again she had found herself in a minority unable to vent her feelings to those around her. Over tea she had berated Onslow again. She had kept her composure but she knew their differences were in danger of undermining their relationship. It was not something she relished. Her mind flashed to the last time they had made love, then to the tenderness of Alfred's lovemaking to Ellie.

She looked across the carriage as it sped silently along. It was far from full which was unusual. A smartly dressed man seated with an equally smart looking attaché case caught her eye. He smiled and she reciprocated but then looked away: she felt no desire to enter into conversation. Instead, in need of escapism she thought of Alfred's plight; his darkest hour, surely she thought as serious in its gravity as 1940. After all, for her hero Alfred, the enemy was already on English soil resplendent and all powerful. If he could somehow turn subjugation into victory and freedom it intrigued her. But there was one thing about which she was sure: he had the vision, the will and the belief to make it happen. How lacking those qualities now seemed in modern Britain. She thought of certain cabinet members whose utterances of desperation only undermined their negotiating hand; a Prime Minister who had voted remain and chosen civil servant colleagues whose only vision was to stay as close to the status quo as possible. What if Alfred had thought likewise? She shuddered at the thought.

Two hours later she stepped into her flat at Kensington. She flicked the light switch and kicked off her shoes. It felt good to be home at last. Her two days in Brussels had been gruelling and depressing in equal measure. She poured a large whisky, threw in a chunk of ice and sipped it gently. Margaret Thatcher she knew had enjoyed scotch; she was in good company! Maggie wondered what she would have said had she been negotiating today.

She turned on the radio. Nigel Farage was in full swing on his LBC show debating with listeners the latest Brexit developments. She listened to callers venting their anger at the Prime Minister's handling of the negotiations. One quoted the words of a German commentator who had demanded 'total surrender' from the British. The caller reminded Farage that the last time total surrender had been demanded by the Germans was at the Battle of the Bulge to which the allied General had replied with a four letter word – NUTS! Farage guffawed in agreement and the point reminded Maggie of what she was witnessing at first hand. If this was a negotiation it certainly didn't feel like it and much of the blame lay on the British side.

She switched off the radio. She had had enough of Brexit for one day. She poured another whisky and sought solace from music. She cast her eye over her impressive collection of discs. Since her student days at Cambridge, Maggie's passion for music had rivalled her passion for history. As she showered, the emotive strains of Sibelius's second symphony wafted through her flat. Why was it her favourite radio programme seemed always to play his fifth she wondered? The second was surely even better in her view.

As the sounds reverberated through her flat she thought just for a moment of her close friend Stella. They had known each other since their Cambridge days. She was a Remainer Maggie knew and that was just fine by her. In fact they had differed little in their outlook. Stella had been willing to accept the majority vote and make the most of whatever new opportunities might lie ahead. Their closeness had remained as intact as ever and the two of them had been able to talk about Brexit in a way that was becoming ever more difficult with Onslow.

For some strange reason Stella reminded her of the sister she had never had. She was precisely the sort of person she imagined the perfect sister would have been – easy going, much in common, even a shared love of history perhaps!

At last as the music of Sibelius had its desired effect Maggie

27

felt herself relax as she took refuge beneath the sheets. In a day or two she would meet with Onslow. She would put her arms around him and restore their relationship she felt sure. Tomorrow would be a better day she told herself as she closed her eyes and let sleep overcome her.

Chapter 3

Summer 2018

The line of EU flags fluttered abreast making their statement outside the Commission upon which the early evening sun had cast a yellow hazy tint. The air was still warm, humid even and the little gusts of breeze offered refreshment to the well dressed Eurocrats emerging from the hallowed ground.

Amongst them a man no more than 5'8", slightly rotund in appearance, the benefactor of fine food and copious imbibing walked slowly away. In his hand he held his mobile phone casually to his ear.

"Yes, I will be with you in 10 minutes at the usual bar. Choose for us a fine bottle of claret my friend and let it air. I will be with you shortly. Goodbye."

Francois Du Bain looked his 55 years and more, a result of fine living made possible by his enormous expenses which he had always claimed without reproach. His greasy, greying hair was combed back and he wore as he always did a pair of expensive black rimmed glasses that gave him an intellectual air; a deception to those who knew him. He had never experienced life in the commercial world preferring to earn his spurs through the Brussels civil service and finally in the bastions of the Commission.

There for the last 7 years he had assumed various mantles determining, sometimes disturbing, the lives of countless millions as his departments' directives had poured forth like a never ending torrent of varying complexity and annoyance to their recipients. Perhaps that was a cynical view but it was the view of one respected British journalist who had challenged him in a TV interview during which Du Bain had assumed an arrogant air and brushed off the criticism, as if the concept of accountability for his actions was totally alien to him.

His career had flourished since that moment. Now his work centred upon the Brexit negotiations, about which he had been obdurate towards his British counterparts. Since Great Britain had had the audacity to vote for the unthinkable, despite the propaganda in which he himself had played no small part, the country would be made to pay – even if European exports were to suffer the consequences. The European project, no matter its imperfections which anyway he denied, could not be seen to be defiled. Punishment would be meted out to any recalcitrant countries considering the same course of action. He had long determined he would show no mercy: negotiation with the British was not a matter of arriving at a win-win outcome; more a matter of simply being intransigent and waiting for the British to give way. So far all was running according to plan. After hearing the British Chancellor's latest comment upon the dire consequences of a no deal, his confidence that all they had to do was sit it out was now sky high.

Minutes later he alighted upon one of his well frequented bars where chairs adorned the edge of the square and happy drinkers sat basking in the evening sun, their Belgian beers upon every table interspersed with bottles of high quality wine. It was a favourite of his Eurocrat friends. A smartly dressed waiter recognised him.

"Bonsoir my friend," Francois said, as he passed by the man. He exuded an air of confidence, if not superiority. The waiter smiled in friendly subservience, eager to accept his next bout of spending. It was then Francois spotted his quarry.

"Onslow my friend," he exclaimed. Onslow Ratcliffe stood up and smiled. He warmly reciprocated an embrace.

"Ah, you have the wine ready. A St. Emilion no less, you cannot go wrong with that!"

Onslow smiled pleased at his friend's approval. He too had emerged from the EU Commission having completed the latest session of exhaustive negotiations. Trading technicalities had been discussed in depth. It had been a sobering experience. Onslow had listened and acquiesced responding to the other side's incessant demands. Francois had as usual kept the momentum going in the EU's favour. Yet the two men had struck up a warm friendship which had not gone unnoticed by the closer observers of protocol.

Francois poured himself a generous glass and sat back in his chair.

"Today was a good day," he announced.

Onslow looked at him. "Good for whom?" he asked rhetorically.

Francois responded immediately, without thought. "Onslow, my dear friend Onslow, yes it was a good day for the EU to be sure, but think what you are gaining! Your trade with us will continue."

Onslow Ratcliffe may have been a fervent Remainer but

this was clearly an absurd statement. Nevertheless he smiled making light of the point. Before he could respond Francois took another swig from his glass and continued unabated.

"I think my friend you should be working here for us, here at the EU!"

Onslow chortled at the suggestion but the warmth between the two men was genuine and perhaps this declaration was sincerely meant.

"Now what makes you say that? I'm happy enough working from London you know."

"Ah, but London is not where you should be. It is here. Here in Brussels, this is where the power now lies. Besides, the rewards are good, very good. We have the highest level of paid holidays anywhere my friend," he boasted.

Onslow sipped his wine whilst continuing to listen. He would not interrupt Francois while he was in full flow.

"Our salaries are very high, our tax rates, well they are how shall I say, very accommodating and our pensions are the best in the world. Well deserved of course!" A smile of satisfaction spread across his features. He drank again from his glass before pouring himself a refill.

"Of course," answered Onslow. "Of course!" The MEPs did even better he knew. He thought of the juicy expenses of almost £4,000 that was paid without question into every MEP's bank account every month. No receipts were required and EU judges had ensured the secretive system would not be exposed to public scrutiny.

For twenty minutes they continued in conversation, every now and again looking around at the scene of relaxed activity as drinkers and diners sought refuge at the end of the working day. The sun had almost disappeared casting deep shadows upon the buildings and shady relief as the temperature had dropped. When their wine was exhausted they ordered two beers. So engrossed in conversation were they that Onslow did not notice the attractive woman who now approached their table.

"Ingrid," called out Francois. The woman dressed in red approached them. She stood at the table and smiled at both men in turn.

She and Francois embraced. She stood upright her hand upon her hip, waiting expectantly to be introduced to Onslow. An expensive figure hugging dress clung to her body displaying her beauty unashamedly. In a trice the Englishman had taken in her blonde, swept back hair and steely blue eyes. Her face was perfectly symmetrical, a picture of sophistication and beauty with an allure about it suggesting there was much to know about this attractive person.

"Let me introduce you Ingrid. This is Onslow Ratcliffe. He is a senior member of the British negotiating team. I don't think you've met." He turned to Onslow. "Ingrid works in my department upon shall we say, somewhat delicate matters."

Onslow kissed her on both cheeks, reciprocating her, and smiled. His eyes locked in on hers.

"Delicate matters?" he enquired.

Francois hesitated and fumbled with his glasses clearly reticent to say more. "Oh, I just meant Ingrid makes herself extremely useful helping the department in all sorts of ways."

She slowly crossed her legs. They were suntanned and toned Onslow noticed. She wore high heels and she let one heel dangle provocatively.

"And how long are you staying Mr Ratcliffe, or may I call you Onslow?" she asked.

Her voice had a sensual quality about it. Onslow had always found English spoken in foreign accents sexy, especially by women from Northern Europe.

"My flight is this evening but I may go tomorrow instead."

Francois interrupted. "Why don't you? Then we can go off to a little club I know, just the three of us."

Ingrid smiled at Onslow and held his gaze. He drew his fingers through his hair. Strangely and without realising it she did the same a few seconds after.

"Excuse me for a moment would you. I just have to make a call," Onslow said. He got up and paced out of earshot, his phone glued to his ear.

"Maggie, how are you? It's Onslow. I'm sorry but I won't now be back until later tomorrow. Something's come up. I'll call you when I'm back, alright?" The call was short and to the point and he quickly resumed his seat.

Later that evening Francois Du Bain was a generous host insisting upon taking them both to an upmarket club he frequented. They sat at a table near the front. A small stage stretched out ahead of them upon which attractive girls, scantily clad, performed dance routines in front of their admiring viewers. As they drank heavily Ingrid enquired more about this man Onslow Ratcliffe as if his role intrigued her. She spoke little of herself but was clearly in awe of her chief, Francois. When the time came to depart she looked at Onslow and leant forward holding her glass provocatively in front of her lips.

"It's been nice meeting you Onslow. Perhaps we shall meet again next time you are in Brussels." She slipped into his hand her business card allowing her fingers a brief moment in time to touch his flesh before losing contact. Onslow gave her no indication of his thoughts other than to smile and when they departed he kissed both of her cheeks before shaking hands with the inebriated Francois.

* * *

The wood panelled office in Whitehall was conducive Maggie thought to clear thinking and creative decision making. It exuded an air of confidence for its occupants what with its high ceilings and capacious splendour. She had attended meetings here before though never she felt in the tense circumstances which now prevailed. She had risen early, intent upon arriving in good time.

"Nice to see you Maggie. We'll commence in five minutes." The voice came from the smartly dressed Sir Stephen Dawkins, a senior civil servant due to chair the meeting.

"Thank you Sir Stephen."

Maggie walked over and stared through one of the enormous windows. She could just see Parliament, dressed as it was in scaffolding as much needed restoration had continued. The sun was beating down. Parliament Square had still looked scorched as she had walked across the grass just minutes before. It felt good to be in the air conditioned luxury of this place.

A dozen or so colleagues had filed in to complete the list of those attending. Onslow was not one of them. She had been understanding of his call delaying his return from Brussels. Nevertheless she still hoped to see him before the day was out.

It was time to take their seats and without due formality Dawkins asked for opinions upon the latest negotiation developments.

"We have to warn the people of the cliff edge if Brussels were to reject the Chequers offer. We have to be prepared. How are we on this?"

For a moment each around the table waited for the other to break the silence.

"Warnings have been prepared and given in regard to various specific issues. We have to prepare people for the worst," a colleague proffered.

Maggie's mind began to race. She thought of Project Fear and the millions of pounds that had been spent in the run up to the referendum to frighten the British people then. Now her colleagues were in danger of doing it all over again. Were more exaggerated negatives to be made of a no deal in the hope they would swallow an offer which kept Britain in the EU in all but name. She heard her name being called.

What is your view Maggie please?" Dawkins asked.

She thought for a moment how to express her view without causing the opprobrium of all her colleagues. She needed she knew to remain restrained, to express herself diplomatically.

"Sir Stephen, I agree that as Cabinet has directed, we must make plans for leaving the EU without an agreement. Indeed being seen by Brussels to do so will strengthen our negotiating hand." Heads nodded at this. She had started well. "However, the public do not trust the government on this. We all know that Project Fear, which let us remind ourselves was funded by the taxpayer at a cost of well over £9 million, was a tendentious falsehood. The economy did not go into immediate recession. Unemployment far from shooting up has reached a four-decade low. Wages are rising at the highest rate for 10 years. Inward investment has done the opposite of what was predicted and third quarter growth is outpacing both Germany and France. Repeating warnings of catastrophe are likely to be seen as simply mendacious."

At this several cries of "No! No!" echoed across the room. But Maggie had not given up quite yet. A third of her colleagues around the table represented the Treasury she realised. Moreover it was the Treasury that had been the principal driver of Project Fear.

"Sir Stephen, only recently the Chancellor supported by the Bank of England has again predicted dire warnings for the economy if a no deal results. Is it not the case that this serves only to weaken our negotiating hand as the EU comes to believe how desperate we are?"

A dramatic silence now descended across the room. For a moment nobody would admit this, least of all those representing the Treasury. Maggie's mind flashed back to the negotiation skills training she had experienced. She knew she was right. Managing expectations in a negotiation was crucially important to maintaining leverage.

A Treasury civil servant now responded. She became animated in her vitriol rejecting Maggie's comments as outrageous. Her odium Maggie suspected, clearly smacked of her overriding need to protect her political masters, regardless of where the truth lay. Maggie determined to press on however.

"Why is it Sir Stephen that we cannot unite around projecting a positive vision for Brexit as many economists say we should? The world is our oyster if only we do not drown ourselves in defeatism."

"What we need," interrupted one of her objectors is pragmatism."

Straight away Maggie blasted back at him. "Pragmatism is a euphemism for defeatism," she declared.

"But we have to remain as close to the EU as possible. Chequers is the solution and we must work upon that basis," another interrupted.

Maggie immediately thought of Alfred; his vision, his absolute determination to bring freedom to his people.

"But we are promoting a vision which is inherently not what the people voted for. We promised them, the Prime Minister promised them, Brexit would be delivered but because our masters – and indeed ourselves have no vision of that, we are delivering Brino instead. Our negotiating needs to switch to a Canada style free trade deal, albeit with the technical solutions to the Irish border that are available, and do so quickly or the Government for whom we serve will never be trusted again. The people Sir Stephen will not have it!"

Again silence reigned in the room. The atmosphere was tense. Maggie looked up. Her eye caught the paintings of Palmerston and Churchill that hung prominently on the opposite wall. Each looked stern and uncompromising. If only her colleagues and political masters would show the same spirit – like Alfred she thought. She looked up at the clock, noting the time at 11.45. Now more of her colleagues who had remained silent were piping up.

The discussions went on, dragging into the afternoon. When eventually Sir Stephen brought the meeting to a close Maggie knew she was in the minority. She consoled herself with the thought that later she would be back in Kensington. She could not wait. She would put on her favourite music. She would kick off her shoes and pour herself a scotch. And above all she would resume where she had left off – reading of Alfred's desperate plight.

Chapter 4

February 878

The ageing peasant was standing in the meadow amidst sheep grazing quietly by. They paid little attention to him recognising him as their shepherd. The grass stretched down to a brook still full with the winter rains. It wound its way along the narrow valley bottom, on the other side of which tall oaks lined the route to a little hamlet. Only a few inhabitants resided here. Not seven years ago the Vikings had ravaged the local villages and their settlement had not been spared. Half its population had been killed. Many of the women folk had been raped some as young as eleven. The Vikings had stolen their horses and raided their stores for provisions before moving on.

The peasant remembered the day as if yesterday. It had scarred his memory leaving an imprint that he knew would remain with him until his dying breath. It had been the year that Alfred after the death of his brother Ethelred had become king. He had chased the Great Heathen Army to Wilton but had been defeated. Somehow he had escaped with his life and forged a truce, but as the Vikings had withdrawn to London they had stopped and laid waste to the peasant's locality.

It was around noon when suddenly the crows circled over-head issuing a raucous incessant cawing as if signalling their displeasure. The peasant looked up at them and back to his sheep. They too were restless and began scurrying back and forth, their heads up, a look of timorous endeavour as if they needed to move but were uncertain in which direction. Then the peasant heard it: the distant sound of horse's hooves carried on the breeze, many of them, thundering towards him. He strained his eyes trying to make out their direction. The noise grew louder. And then he saw them; perhaps twenty or thirty riders galloping furiously. They were coming closer, hugging the side of the valley keeping below the sight line of the ridge. He tensed as they drew closer. The thought it could be the Vikings again did not escape him.

Spotting the brook Alfred and Ellie brought their exhausted horses to a halt. Quickly they dismounted. As the horses drank from the flowing stream he knelt down and threw the cold water over his head. It felt good. He cupped his hands and offered water up to Ellie's lips. She drank quickly holding his fingers as she did so. The memory of their midnight escape from Chippenham now several weeks before still frightened her. They had ridden hard pausing to hide at regular intervals. Around them the small retinue of Alfred's warriors who had fled with them tended to their horses. One of them came and stood beside Alfred.

"Sire, the Vikings may be close. We dare not tarry long."

"We will ride all the better for letting the horses drink and rest just for a short while. The sun is high. It must be noon. We need to move farther west towards Somerset. Tell the men we keep riding into the sun and keeping to the lower ground before hiding once again."

He looked at Ellie and pulled her calmly to him. He hugged her; an embrace that spoke of comfort, of confidence that they would make their escape and elude Guthrum yet again. He kissed her gently.

"We will make it my love. I promise you. Have faith." He squeezed her hand as if to emphasise his words. But he was all too well aware the Great Viking Army so determined to remove him from the throne of Wessex would not be far behind. Alfred looked around. His keen eye noticed the old peasant keeping his distance. He walked over to him.

"Do not be afraid, we are friends not foes," he called as he drew close. The peasant looked at him warily. Alfred had disguised himself in an old smock giving no indication he was this man's king and sovereign. The fellow did not turn away. Alfred smiled a look of reassurance.

"Pray tell me, where does this valley lead to?" he asked him.

The peasant hesitated, then raised his arm pointing towards the sun. "To the flat levels thence to the Tor, the great Tor of Glastonbury," he uttered.

Alfred bade him well. He still did not reveal himself. The fewer people who knew he had passed this way the better.

He walked briskly back to the others. "We must keep going. Let us ride and bestow ourselves with speed," he commanded them.

In a moment they had galloped off along the valley, the old peasant watching as they sped into the distance. These strange men in such a hurry, he wondered, who were they?

It was sometime later he caught the distant sight of horses once again. He peered out of his tiny shack up across the brook. Above the tall dark oaks that lined the narrow valley he saw what looked like mounted warriors on the skyline moving south. Instantly, he felt his stomach tightening in a knot as fear shot through him. Something instinctively suggested these were Vikings but he could not be certain. Soon after he could see warriors on foot some wearing helmets, the sunshine reflecting upon their swords and round metal shields. They were fighting men alright – and yes, they might well be what he feared. Thank God they passed by without descending down the valley.

Days later Alfred and his motley retinue had ridden several miles on, hiding at times then riding when it was safe to do so. The ground was softer and wetter now, the longer grass slowing their progress. Every now and again Alfred would look back straining his eye to search for their assailants. Still he saw nothing as yet. Ahead green meadows spread out in front of them; a great tapestry of beauty, intersected by gentle slopes of undulating hills and beyond them the beginnings of the Somerset levels. The low afternoon sun lent the scene a special shade of green. It was a calming, consoling sight he thought; a false suggestion of serenity, of a tranquil peaceful land.

No sooner had his mind relaxed, the stark contrast with reality overcame him of the awful situation in which they had found themselves. And then in a moment the great Tor of Glastonbury came into view standing resplendently like a sentry above the surrounding land as if everything around was paying homage in respect of its power and presence.

Ellie allowed herself the briefest of smiles as she took in the distant sight. She cast a glance at Alfred as she rode beside him. They were making good progress now she convinced herself. Her mind flashed back to their last night in Chippenham: to their making love; to how she had listened enraptured as he had shared with her his dreams. She remembered too how she had lain in his arms and listened to his breathing as that evening had taken hold. It seemed a lifetime away.

That night Alfred decided to pause and hide once again but only till the first hints of dawn broke the darkness. He tossed and turned, trying not to wake Ellie who lay exhausted beside him.

His spies had alerted him of another Viking Army led by Ubba, the surviving son of the infamous Viking king, Ragnar Lothbrok. It had been Ubba who had laid waste to East Anglia eight years previously and who had slain the brave King Edmund. As he lay turning in his half sleep the words of Edgar, his faithful but sometimes defeatist spy flashed through his mind: Edgar's intelligence deemed from captured patrols had told of Ubba bringing his ships and men from Dublin to bear down upon Wessex from the west. But where were they now Alfred pondered? The last thing he needed was to be caught in a pincer movement between Guthrum to the north and Ubba from the west. His eye was set upon reaching Athelney, his royal hunting lodge remotely hidden amidst the marshes of Somerset. If he could make it to Athelney over the coming days and weeks then surely he could elude the Vikings once again.

As first light broke, he ordered three of his men to ride to Countisbury in Devon where he knew a sizeable force of West Saxons was based. They were to gain news of the advance of Ubba and bring it to him at Athelney he commanded them.

As they set off Alfred gathered his faithful warriors

together. There were small Viking bases he told them, spread along their route which the Great Army on their tail would use to shore up and consolidate their strength as they advanced south. From now on as Alfred's men moved slowly west towards the Somerset levels, they would make it their business he told them, to raid these bases wherever they came across them. His tactics would not be those of an army, not for the moment anyway, but those of a small undetectable guerrilla unit constantly raiding and then hiding from detection.

They would inflict damage upon their enemy undermining Guthrum, frustrating him at every turn. They would Alfred told them, not be vanquished. They would never surrender. This was to be a calculated retreat not a rout. No hint of defeatism would be allowed. They would turn that retreat to advantage by attacking them whenever the opportunity arose, lying low in hiding and then repeating the process.

As they reached eventually the great Tor of Glastonbury a new confidence pervaded through his intrepid followers. The awful fear that had haunted them was changing; not gone, but certainly diminished, transformed motivationally into a belief that in the end with God's help they would prevail. They might still be caught each man knew, but they would rather choke in their own blood than surrender. They would somehow turn their situation around and this was the beginning. Defiance would be their watchword; defiance would be their unstinting aim, their focus and their resolve.

One day victory would come, victory borne out of their suffering, victory borne out of their steadfast defiance; victory secured no matter how long and tortuous the road may be.

March 878

Ellie stood quite still and looked out across the near impassable swampy marshes that characterised this remote part of the Somerset levels. The high point that marked one end of their small hill fort offered an enchanting view she thought. Below lay the confluence of the rivers Parrett and Tone that meandered unhurriedly across the valley, behind which another small hill stood commandingly, high above the marshes. She turned and looked across the little dwellings that nestled together within the fort confines. The ditch below the steep bank with the palisade above looked formidable enough she thought. As she stood alone she allowed herself a prayer that she would never witness putting their humble defences to the test.

Christmas at Chippenham now seemed long since past. Already it was late March in this fateful year of 878. They had lain in hiding for over two months evading being spotted by the Vikings or their acquiescent lackeys. Those cold winter months had been truly Alfred's darkest hour. At least now at last at Athelney there was a semblance of safety provided no one saw through their disguise. Alfred's identity had to remain a secret except to those few with whom he had escaped Chippenham.

As Ellie had strolled earlier, close to the marsh, she had noticed the early signs of spring: bright green shoots springing up through the dead rushes; crisp clean spring air with just a hint of warmth, thank God, and signs of new life from insects skating across the quiet waters imperceptible to the non observant. But Ellie was observant. She took in all around her, often pointing things out to Alfred who found her perceptive, perspicacious nature as alluring as her physical presence. She turned as he approached and took him by the hand.

Slowly she led him along the top of the bank. She gazed at two horses, their heads bowed as they chewed the grass oblivious to their passing. The distant sound of voices in friendly conversation could be heard. Just for a moment Ellie felt the sense of imminent danger leave her. No doubt it would return but today, perhaps today at least she could think of other things. She looked up at Alfred and squeezed his hand.

"Tell me about your boyhood," she asked. "What do you remember?"

Alfred thought for a moment, puzzled by her question but intrigued she wanted to know.

"I was born in Wantage in 849." He hesitated, wondering what he should reveal. He held no secrets from her but had no wish to bore her with his past.

"I suppose what I remember the most was going to Rome when I was just a few years old," he continued. His eyes looked up recalling the vivid images, scenes that had never left him. She detected a hint of a smile as the memories flooded back.

"Rome?" she pressed him.

Alfred gazed into the distance as he spoke. "My father, King Ethelwulf dispatched myself and my elder brother Ethelred there. It was a pilgrimage. My father had arranged safe passage for us. It was a magical time Ellie."

"Did you meet the Pope? What happened to you there?" She clutched his arm encouraging him to open up to her as they strolled slowly on. Again Alfred took his time before answering.

"There was a Saxon school not far from the Vatican. I was honoured by the Pope, Pope Leo IV. I learnt more of Christ and my beliefs grew at that time – his teaching is the basis of what I want to give my people, do you see?"

Before she could answer he continued. "Rules for living in the way our Father in heaven intended – the Ten Commandments. Without good rules written into Godly laws all is lost I believe." Alfred paused again as he spoke, recalling the emotions of what the experience had meant to him at such a young age. "A year or two later I returned to Rome, this time with my father as well. That is when he met his second wife, my stepmother Judith."

He gazed up and stared across the marshy vista. Below them a heron was wading at the water's edge.

"What happened to your real mother Alfred, what happened to her?" Ellie persisted.

"She died when I was very young. My father, my mother, my brothers, all have now died." Alfred swallowed as a wave of emotion overtook him. Ellie sensed it and hugged him. She loved this man she thought, a brave warrior and clever commander of his followers but what moved her was his vulnerability; his unselfish caring nature that stood in contrast to the cold ruthlessness of their pagan oppressors. How fortunate the people of Wessex were to have her lover as their leader she mused.

Later that day as they huddled together beside a fire Alfred spoke more to her of his past and that of his beloved Wessex. He explained how those before him had succumbed to the paying of protection money to the Vikings, endless payments that would come to be known as Danegeld. Always it had bought peace for a while. The Vikings saw it as ready income to be demanded whenever they pleased. But they had only been able to do so because his countrymen had not had the will and the strategy to defy them.

But those payments would no longer be made he explained. He would concede no more and force the issue through demonstrating strength rather than weakness. They had been through three months of hell. But his vision had not been diminished, not one iota. Somehow out of this darkest hour with the hand of providence upon him, he would again lead a united army sharing his vision of freedom: as a result they would exert leverage over the Vikings, forcing them into a negotiated settlement.

As Alfred talked into the evening Ellie listened intrigued by what she heard and when sleep took hold she nestled in his arms and dreamed of such a peace. He had unknowingly given her something she had craved – hope, and a confidence that no matter how dire their situation now was, somehow his dream would indeed be turned to reality.

Chapter 5

Summer 2018

It had been several days since Onslow had called Maggie from Brussels to delay their meeting together. For whatever reason their paths had not crossed in Whitehall. Maggie guessed he had been preoccupied with the complexities of a myriad of technical aspects that were the foundation for any negotiated deal. Their argument the last time she had seen him still lingered in her mind. His right to disagree was not in question: it was the sense that her view met with an almost disparaging response that smacked of smugness that she minded most. Not only that but her absolute conviction that what they were about was essentially a deceitful rebuke to the wishes of the people. Yet she had no wish to allow their work on Brexit to sour their relationship. She still found him attractive and anyway the relationship was still young. She barely knew the real Onslow Ratcliffe.

He had called her during the afternoon promising a surprise. He offered no explanation leaving Maggie in a state of expectancy as she watched out of the window for his car. She looked at her watch. He was already overdue but not by much. She glanced outside again and it was then she spotted the red Porsche pulling up. She waited for the bell to ring.

Determined not to appear too keen she then counted to ten before opening the door. He stood in front of her and smiled. In his hands he held a bouquet of flowers.

"Peace offering?" she asked him. She watched him hesitate not quite certain how to respond. She remained silent putting pressure upon him just as she had learned in her negotiation training.

"Peace offering," he replied. He embraced her and she led him into the lounge.

"It's good to see you Onslow." She kissed him on the cheek before turning away and pouring him a cold beer. "Perhaps you could do with this," she said.

He grinned and drank from the glass. "Maggie, let's not fall out over our work together. We both have to deal with the negotiations. Let's stay on the same side, eh?"

In the flash of a second she felt the need to respond. She knew all too well to which side he was referring. But she kept her mouth shut determined this time to avoid another argument. Too many friendships had already been broken over the issue and she had no intention of following suit.

"Let's talk of other things," she replied, avoiding a direct answer to his question.

He reached inside his pocket and pulled out what looked like two tickets.

"I have a surprise for you Maggie," he declared. "I know how you love your classical music. The Proms have ended as you know but there's a concert tonight. I have two tickets for the Albert Hall. How does that sound?"

Maggie could not conceal her delight. She put her arms around Onslow and kissed him.

A little later they walked out of the flat down Kensington

Church Street turning left into the High Street. The warmth of the day had given way to the coolness of the early evening. Now in late September the first hints of crisp autumnal air were becoming apparent. They walked holding hands passed the Royal Garden Hotel and soon after entered the hallowed portals of this most majestic of concert halls. As they took their seats in the front row directly below the conductor Maggie took Onslow's hand in hers.

"Thank you," she said. "I so love this place. Thank you Onslow for a lovely surprise." As the words flowed from her lips she felt the need to kiss him. She leant toward him allowing her lips to touch his and her hand to pass over his thigh. He looked at her and smiled. Now their relationship was back on track she mused.

But this was the Royal Albert Hall and she had no wish to be other than discreet. Quickly she sat back in her seat without though letting go of his hand and waited for the proceedings to begin. Minutes later Tchaikovsky's magnificent violin concerto resounded through the great auditorium. She sat transfixed, totally immersed in the glorious sound, intent only upon letting the music wash over her. When it ended the entire hall erupted with loud applause. Maggie Taylor clapped as energetically as anybody. She grinned with pleasure. What a wonderful evening this was she thought. She felt herself gripping Onslow's hand harder. She squeezed his fingers in her delight waiting with excited anticipation for what was to follow. It was one of her favourites – Grieg's piano concerto in A minor.

In a moment the conductor had taken his place and as the pianist walked serenely to the grand piano just feet in front of them the audience broke into more spontaneous applause.

She glanced quickly at Onslow as if to confirm he shared her excitement.

She was beautiful Onslow thought as the concert pianist stood in front of them. He looked carefully up at her. Her blonde hair hung loosely about her shoulders. The ends were curled provocatively as if inviting hands to pass through, perhaps her own hands, perhaps the hands of her lover, who knows. She wore a deep grey skin tight dress which clung to a perfect figure. Her skin was tanned though not overly so, her face beautiful and enchantingly seductive. Onslow watched mesmerised as she lowered herself on to the piano stool not feet away from them.

She steadied herself, moving her hips carefully into the most comfortable position before the intense excitement of the opening notes. He watched as suddenly her forearms hammered down upon the submissive keys. Soon the excitement of the opening bars gave way to contrast. Suddenly her movements slowed, her hands now moving with the utmost tenderness, slowly, ever so slowly stroking the keys. Now her head was thrust back, her slender body arched back once more succumbing to the exquisiteness of the music, dormant now, subdued, played tantalisingly slowly giving no clue as to the expectation of what was to follow. He watched the expression of bliss upon her face, her hair thrown back now, her eyes closed as her hands nonchalantly worked the keyboard sending sensations of pleasure running through her.

But it was not her face above him that Onslow saw as he sat mesmerised. It was not the face of Maggie either. It was the face of Ingrid he imagined; her high cheek bones, her hair tossed back as she fed upon her pleasure. As the slow sensuous notes continued, she raised her face toward the heavens wavering gently to the right and then to the left, her eyes still closed in a world of her own; a world she never wanted to end. Onslow could feel himself entranced by what he was watching, imagining it was Ingrid astride him. If ever he needed proof that music could arouse the most erotic feelings he needed now no convincing. But he was unable to resist. The sight, the sounds were simply too alluring. He gave in and surrendered himself to it just as this beautiful pianist was giving in to her pleasure also.

He waited now for what was to come. He knew the piece well. Deliberately he was convinced, she was holding it back, playing with the notes subtlety, tantalisingly slowly, holding Grieg's climax that was to come in captivity, tying it down waiting to be unleashed. The tension seemed unbearable; a dam waiting to give way to an unstoppable torrent as the walls of resistance finally gave way. And then it came.

Suddenly her forearms began moving faster, not instantly but accelerating, abandoned uninhibitedly to what Grieg intended: then working the keys at an incredible speed, her head suddenly down, her hair hanging almost touching the keyboard as her fingers pummelled the keys into submission wringing from them Grieg's loud explosive climax. Onslow watched, his imagination on fire. To him it was Ingrid he was watching still, unable to shift her from his mind. Now as if convulsions overcame her she raised herself from the stool taking her weight upon her thighs, her head bowing uncontrollably over the keys, her eyes still closed as she bathed in her pleasure.

Later that evening when they made love Maggie writhed in Onslow's arms but deep down for some unknown, unfathomable reason her mood had changed.

* * *

At Cambridge Maggie had formed a close relationship with a fellow student who like her had gained a double first. Stella Lawton was one of those people with whom Maggie could feel totally relaxed and when she had called to ask if she fancied a weekend in the Dordogne she had readily consented. Besides she needed time away from London, away from the Brexit negotiations and perhaps she instinctively felt, a little time apart from Onslow. So it was that two days later they met at Heathrow and when their plane touched down at Bergerac her mood of recent days had lifted.

They hired a car and headed south to the little place she had booked near Eymet. She hadn't seen Stella for a while but she had not changed. Still the engaging smile, the happy disposition and the loose limbed athleticism which she brought to every physical activity. She had been sporting at Cambridge. Now at 34 she had kept her figure and to Maggie's eye looked radiant.

The journey was short and Maggie was in no hurry. This was bastide country – the myriad of beautiful little towns dating back to before the Hundred Years War with the English. She had spent time here as a teenager entranced by the exquisite beauty of the old buildings nestled together as if protecting one another from the passage of time, not to mention various wars and occupation. No modern architect could conceivably have designed these little towns with their oddly shaped timber and stone constructions, the antithesis of the precise lines of modern structures. In their rough hewn grey stone with a subtle tint of gold, each house somehow still stood, asserting proudly and magnificently

54

the skills of their medieval builders. At their centre cobbled streets gave way to wide open squares demanding every onlooker to turn aghast 360 degrees to take in the beauty. Great stone arches acted as partitions beneath which little French cafes announced their attractions to passersby. As they drove slowly, Maggie could have been forgiven for taking her eye off the road.

Between each bastide town the narrow country roads meandered along, the pace of life determined only by farmers going about their business. But just as in medieval days the English love, or was it possession, of the area was still intact. Forty percent of the population of Eymet were English, Maggie knew. It remained a magnet for British holiday makers of a certain persuasion. But these were not the drunk Brits that plagued other shores: the visitors here were altogether more respectful, refined and cultured, with genteel manners and a love of the Dordogne, fine food and fine wine.

As they chatted, Stella commented upon the lack of traffic compared to British roads. Just for a moment the subject of Brexit entered Maggie's head. She felt powerless to stop her mind reverting to it. How ironic it was she thought that under the previous Labour government immigration to the small island that was her home had deliberately been allowed to rise exponentially – and yet this had come back to haunt the establishment Remainers as voters at the referendum had taken their revenge. She thought of the negotiations in which she was immersed: little would change she knew as concessions were made.

Her restless mind switched back to the beauty surrounding them as they drove on. This was not the hedge lined bocage of Normandy but it held similarities nevertheless. Gently undulating fields broken up with idyllic stone farmhouses and barns similar to the Devon long barns that Maggie knew. The quiet bucolic landscape little changed over the centuries made her think of her music; Beethoven's Pastoral could have been written for these views she ruminated.

That evening they dined at a little bistro at Beaumont and afterwards they chatted into the early hours. Maggie slept better than for a long time and when she rose late she found Stella was already up but nowhere to be seen. She ventured outside. Their cottage had a small pool surrounded by loungers and umbrellas that had seen better days. The lithe bikini clad figure of her friend was moving serenely through the water. Maggie watched for a moment admiring her crawl: there was an elegance to it, a slow rhythmic stroke which propelled Stella effortlessly along the pool. She dipped her hand in. The water felt warm and for the rest of the day they swam and relaxed, chatting about this and that but never about Brexit.

During the afternoon she took a call from Onslow. His tone was warm, but the conversation was brief. She put the phone down. Stella sensed Maggie's reaction.

"Come on, tell me about it over dinner," she said.

Maggie smiled. She could talk openly to Stella. Perhaps she would share her thoughts later but in all honesty she was not sure herself of her feelings. A glass or two of wine would help.

Later they drove to Monpazier, in Maggie's opinion the finest of the bastide towns. She remembered it well from her earlier visits. Of course it had not changed. To have even suggested such a thing would have been to insult this singularly beautiful town. Surely it had barely changed since its inception under King Edward 1st in 1284 when its medieval architect had set out the grid system upon a roll of parchment. The two women looked at each other expectantly as one of the great arched entrances sprang into view. Lined up on each side stood ancient stone houses acting as defensive walls. No Hollywood movie could replicate such a sight.

Minutes later they strolled through another arch some 24 feet deep. Together they sauntered down the Rue Notre Dame between old stone walled dwellings with shuttered windows stretching back into antiquity. When they reached the Place des Cornieres, the sublime central square, they stood in awe for several moments. At its centre was Les Halles, the covered market supported by ancient timbers set at regular intervals resembling a pagoda from medieval times. Maggie stared at the arches of varying size and shape that bordered each side of the square. Unlike Eymet there were no timbered beams spreading like tentacles in whatever disparate direction had taken the builders' fancy. The arches instead seemed to her to resemble a painting in which the artist cared nothing for conformity but revelled in the audacity of being uncompromisingly distinctive and beautiful in equal measure. Above them colourful flowers draped from balconies, aside little windows framed by old timbered shutters.

Stella looked at her watch. It was time to dine and the light was fading fast though still warm enough to eat outside. Together they retraced their footsteps past L'Eglise Saint Dominique and took a table in the courtyard of the Privilege du Perigord. The restaurant had a relaxing ambience.

57

Hanging baskets hung from the walls, intermingled with old lamps that cast a gentle light upon the scene. The two women surveyed the menu. Both fancied duck and ordered Cuisse de Lapereau Confite and a carafe of Bergerac red.

The waiter was good looking Maggie couldn't help noticing and charming with it. He looked at them each in turn and grinned. "You will enjoy your meal," he said. Maggie listened to his endearing French accent. It had a romantic charm she could not deny.

"You like him, I can tell. Don't try to hide it," Stella whispered to her.

Maggie grinned but said nothing.

"You haven't told me about Onslow. Are you happy together?" Stella knew she was being direct but was certain Maggie needed to open up. She hesitated before answering.

"We've been seeing each other for just two months Stella. It's not long, you know." She sipped her wine before allowing herself to confide in her friend.

"Onslow and I are working closely together in the Brexit negotiations. I cannot say too much, you understand." Stella nodded.

"I've come to realise we have different beliefs over Brexit. We are supposed to be impartial simply doing what our political masters tell us but ..." She hesitated before continuing. "But I am in a minority and it causes difficulty between us."

Stella leant forward cupping her glass. "I am a Remainer Maggie, but the Leavers won the referendum and we were promised the majority vote would be respected by Cameron. But there are many Remainers who simply won't accept the result and will do anything to frustrate the will of the people even insisting upon a second referendum – I call the House of Lords the House of Vichy now! All I want to do is get on with it. If the people's will is to make us global and independent then let's unite and take advantage and get on with it!"

"Tell me about it," Maggie responded. She sipped again from her glass and stared intently at her friend. "Can I tell you something in confidence and please whatever you do, do not repeat this to anyone." Stella looked surprised, unsure of what was to emanate from Maggie's lips.

"I'm not sure what to do. We are under orders from Downing Street to negotiate the Chequers offer on the grounds it delivers Brexit but we all know it does nothing of the sort. It is a deceit, a complete and utter deceit. Yet my colleagues are happy to go along with it. What on earth am I to do?"

Stella looked first at Maggie then at the empty carafe. "I think we need another," she said. She beckoned to the waiter. The hint of a grin spread across her face as she attempted to lighten the conversation. Another carafe was quickly put in front of them. The waiter smiled. Maggie chose to ignore his eye contact, too immersed in their conversation to be distracted.

"Stella, we've given away too much, you wouldn't believe it. The PM went to visit Macron a little while ago. Whether it was to plead or negotiate is a moot point. It's an absolute humiliation. A complete humiliation and yet we are all expected to just go along with it. It's a conspiracy, a conspiracy I tell you."

She stopped herself from saying anymore. She had said too much already she knew. The fine French wine had loosened her tongue but her need to spill out her feelings to her old and trusted friend felt overwhelming. "I feel like going to the press, but I would be in terrible trouble if I disclosed what I know." Again she stopped, arrested by her own rhetoric. Stella had listened intently to this. She was a business woman not a politician but had remained well informed.

"Maggie believe me I know. The Telegraph has been inundated with a thousand letters or more from people objecting to the sell out of Chequers. The Tories have lost swathes of supporters, though many more are joining up to vote in a new PM when the leadership election comes. The trouble is many of the constituency chairmen have been given succour and sherry at Downing Street and are going along with it. Meanwhile Farage is openly calling the PM, Theresa the appeaser. But some of the chairmen just don't get it."

Stella poured herself another generous glass. She leant across and touched Maggie on the arm. She continued calmly choosing her words carefully.

"The will of the people must be carried out and your duty is to try to do it, no matter what it takes."

"But what do I do? If I speak up about what is happening I could lose my job." Stella held her by her hand again. Maggie sounded exasperated. She had never heard her speak in this way.

"Maggie, you know I studied modern history when we were together at Cambridge. Well those who stood up against Chamberlain's appeasement were given a very hard time, not least by the then Chief Whip, David Margesson. History is simply repeating itself. It's the same thing all over again."

"If history is repeating itself, then where is the Churchill?"

Stella looked perplexed before answering. "They are all the

descendants of Churchill's nemesis, Halifax," she declared, half in jest. "Come to think of it, Boris is like Churchill in some ways; clever, outspoken and popular with the people but less popular with the MPs."

Stella looked away for a moment noticing how the lamps had cast a softer glow as the darkness had descended. It was good to be able to dine outside she thought.

"Can I tell you something?" Maggie interrupted. "I truly believe that if the people don't get what they voted for they will never forgive us. They are restive Stella, restive. This is the most dangerous situation since the civil war over 350 years ago and the government is entirely to blame."

Stella sipped from her glass. She looked around at the happy people surrounding them, each in pleasant conversation unaware of the seriousness of their own discussion. The waiter appeared again from nowhere. Once again both women avoided eye contact but watched as he lit a candle between them.

"Is everything alright?" he asked.

"Yes thank you," Stella replied briskly. She turned again to her friend immediately he walked away. But Maggie said nothing. She had said far too much already to the one person she could confide in.

In due course they left the restaurant. Stella had been a good listener but now Maggie vowed not to speak of her work in Whitehall any further. The next day they drove east and walked the narrow passages of the impossibly beautiful town of Sarlat. With every step Maggie felt a curious sense of escapism that was not lost on her perceptive friend. Later they took coffee at the medieval cliff top town of Domme.

It was the next day when they sat side by side on the plane

back to London Stella noticed the open book upon Maggie's lap.

"What are you reading?" she enquired.

Maggie looked up. "The story of King Alfred," she replied. She began to explain what she had read. Stella detected the change in her tone as her enthusiasm rose.

"You mentioned Churchill the other night," Maggie said. "But you know Churchill himself confessed that the greatest Englishman was not himself but Alfred the Great!"

A hint of a smile spread across Stella's face. She looked at her friend. "I think you are actually just a little bit in love with him," she said.

"Perhaps I am," replied Maggie. "Perhaps I am."

Chapter 6

April 878

Alfred had quietly slipped away from the tiny hill fort at Athelney that had become home for him and Ellie, and the small retinue of warriors who had ridden with him. He needed solace; time to think alone and he had found it as he walked a mile or so to the little neighbouring settlement. Still in his smock giving no hint of his royal person, he had engaged a swineherd and his wife in conversation. They had offered the stranger a drink and showed him into their humble dwelling. The woman had been baking cakes and had promised Alfred that he could partake of them once ready. He had accepted their kindness graciously and when she asked him to oversee the baking as she had been called to an errand he bowed to her request.

Now sat over the fire alone he looked up startled by a bird of prey that hovered nearby. The afternoon sky seemed to him the purist blue, broken only by high clouds wafting slowly from the west. And it was from the west that at last good news had reached him. A smile spread across Alfred's handsome features as he played over in his mind the ramifications of the reports he had received.

Instead of joining Guthrum's Great Army, the Viking

army that had sailed from Dublin led by Ubba had arrived in Wales where they had plundered and slaughtered without mercy. From there they had crossed to Devon in two dozen longships. There they had been confronted by a sizeable force of West Saxons led by their Alderman, whose name was Odda. He had launched an attack from their base near Countisbury and with the element of surprise on his side had won a significant victory. Nearly a thousand Vikings had been killed. Ubba himself had been slain.

Alfred glanced down at the cakes as he ruminated upon the good tidings. He had never baked cakes in his life but they were he judged, doing nicely. He closed his eyes and focussed his mind again upon what the news meant. Guthrum would no doubt be hugely frustrated that his grand pincer movement was now in tatters. Not only that but if the Viking Army of Ubba could be defeated in Devon then surely he, Alfred, could turn their defiance into an eventual victory – a victory that would as he had dreamed free all of Wessex.

The Vikings could be beaten! After all, he and his brother Ethelred had beaten them at Ashdown: his mind swirled back to their great battle in 871. The memories had never left him; that cold morning not far from Marlborough; his estate at Wallingford that had been their base; the commands he had given to close the shield wall and charge the enemy putting them to flight. He remembered still the moment the Viking wall had broken and in the aftermath how he had counted the scores of blood-soaked bodies as they lay upon the Berkshire Downs. He remembered too the cries of men dying from their wounds, their entrails laid bare, their limbs torn from them crying out for their mothers in their torment. The sounds still haunted him.

Alfred had been in a score of battles. But it was at Ashdown he had earned his spurs. He had become the crucial commander, the role that history had determined for him. And what destiny commanded, he would now as then obey.

Yet for now as for the last three months, he was a fugitive. He had eluded Guthrum once again but his motivation driven by his passionate belief in the book of Psalms had kept him going. After all, David their author had himself been a fugitive. Alfred could see the similarities between them and took encouragement.

He looked up, his thoughts broken by the bird of prey that had returned and hovered again looking for its next meal. How cruel nature was Alfred thought. He cast his eye across the fields. The sun had now given them a hazy shade of green, the definition of trees on the skyline difficult to make out. Somewhere back there, somewhere through those trees he mused, Guthrum was still there looking for them.

Alfred had sent raiding parties to harry their bases. Sometimes though not always they had brought news of The Great Army's whereabouts. He remained confident however, that for the moment anyway, he had eluded them.

His thoughts turned back to the news from Devon. Not only had Ubba been beaten but their raven banner that struck fear into the hearts of their enemies had been captured. To the Vikings this was of immense importance. That day the banner with its woven ravens' wings had hung lifeless, a portent of their defeat. Their morale had taken a battering as a result. Alfred had good reason to feel his mood uplifted as he sat lost in thought. Suddenly the silence was shattered however. The swineherd's wife had returned.

"What have you done to my cakes?" she demanded. "They

are burnt, you silly man. Burnt, can't you see?" She slapped Alfred across his shoulder. Her face, kindly before, had assumed a haggard, cross look of annoyance. She slapped him a second time. It was all Alfred could do to apologise profusely and make his way from the place.

Later he sat with Ellie and told her what had happened. She laughed aloud and threw her arms around him.

"My poor Alfred," she said. "You are my fearless warrior. Yet you humble yourself before God and you let yourself be scolded by a swineherd's wife while you plan our freedom. You are some man my darling. I love you so much."

Summer 2018

Maggie put her book down. A tear filled her eye as she pictured the scene. Stella's words had remained with her. Perhaps indeed she would have loved this man; perhaps she would have vied with Ellie for him. Her mind was now however, upon the daunting day ahead.

A meeting had been planned in Brussels but at the last minute had been moved to London. It had been put to Sir Stephen Dawkins that a minimum of discussion should be given as to how to fend off the pressure building from within the Tory ranks for a Canada style free trade deal. Downing Street had been adamant this would not be countenanced but the arguments as to why had to be prepared, not least ahead of the imminent Tory party conference. 2018 promised, Maggie knew, to be the most turbulent autumn in British politics for many a year.

When she arrived at the same oak panelled room they

had met in just a little time ago, she was as previously greeted courteously by Sir Stephen. He had an innate charm about him that Maggie respected, though remained wary of. Somehow with a woman's perception she had come to realise the incongruency between his words and his facial expression. His true meaning she knew only too well lay in the latter.

She looked across the large mahogany table. She knew all the familiar faces. Onslow sat directly opposite Sir Stephen. She had been unaware he was to attend the same meeting. He smiled at her and the memories of their recent date at the Royal Albert Hall for a brief moment flooded back. The thought of how long their peace over Brexit would last had lapsed in her mind: it was something else that she could not put her finger on that concerned her.

Sir Stephen called the meeting to order. He spoke coherently, choosing his words as he always did with the utmost care. It was after all the hallmark of his profession: the art of speaking in the most diplomatic manner whilst advocating a different view so subtly the listener hardly realised. Maggie had read of the studies from the USA about the skills of chairmanship: how a good chairman or madam chairman maintained a certain reservation in projecting their views whilst others allowed their personal views to take centre stage. When those gathered had given way to the latter, Maggie knew the quality of decision making was invariably poorer, though instances she could think of in history not least concerning Thatcher and Churchill, occasionally overrode the rule.

"We are required to assess a suitable response to those who are now advocating a Canada style free trade agreement instead of the Chequers offer. We all know Downing

Street's take on this. May I have your opinions beginning with regulatory divergence please?" Dawkins paused and looked around the table.

"Under Canada Plus we would be permitted to change our regulations in the future. Under Chequers we could not attempt to make ourselves more competitive. It is difficult to argue against that," said one.

Maggie nodded in agreement.

"And what about the Irish border?" interrupted Onslow. "Under Chequers we would remain aligned with EU rules with no need for a hard border. With a Canada style free trade agreement a hard border would be needed which is unacceptable to the EU."

Maggie now intervened. "Only because we have foolishly agreed to the Irish backstop," she declared. "However, Onslow with respect is wrong. Trusted trader schemes and new technology would ensure no hard border. Where there's a will there's a way," she declared.

"Then what about trade deals?" enquired Sir Stephen.

"There would be no restrictions under the Canada option upon lucrative free trade deals being negotiated by us and that would give us huge opportunities with the Asian countries not to mention China, the US and India, there is no denying it. As we all should admit, the common rule book under Chequers makes trade deals all but impossible." It was the same senior civil servant who had spoken previously, Crispin Urquart. Again Maggie nodded in agreement. She had one ally anyway she realised.

It was the voice of Onslow that she heard next. "But our instructions are to defend Chequers so we must keep quiet about what we know."

Maggie glared at him across the table and retorted immediately.

"Ah, you mean pretend these are unknown unknowns as Donald Rumsfeld would say, Johari's principle." She was not certain quite how many of her colleagues were familiar with Johari's principle but it was an apt description of what to her mind amounted to rank dishonesty. She instantly decided to pour more salt into the wound.

"Are we suggesting we should also bury the truth in regard to immigration since the Canada option gives complete freedom on policy which Chequers will not when we have made more concessions as we undoubtedly will?" she added. "The same goes in regard to control by the European Court of Justice. Under Chequers we are under their control, under Canada we are in control! Are we to bury the truth on that too?"

A deathly silence filled the room. For several moments no one uttered a word. It was Onslow again who spoke first.

"Our directive is to counter these arguments. Maggie may have a point but our advice in support of Downing Street must be to stick to the line that to do anything other than remain tied to Europe would be foolish. We must suggest the alternatives are too hideous to even consider. Clearly most elements of the establishment and media are supporting us. The Treasury will support us too, I have no doubt."

Maggie looked aghast. His acknowledgment to her sounded more than a touch patronising. But Onslow had not finished yet.

"Downing Street will concede more on the European Court of Justice, on freedom of movement and indeed on the customs union and our advice should be to do precisely that." He looked around the room as if pleading for support from his colleagues. "But we can camouflage it sufficiently with the help of the EU so the violation of our red lines is disguised. I can explore this with my contacts in Brussels if that is helpful."

The tension was now palpable and tempers were beginning to fray. Sir Stephen intervened in support of Onslow.

"That is right. We must get Chequers accepted even if we have to make more concessions and payments to the EU. That is the answer. Talk to your contacts in Brussels Onslow. We must get it agreed. No matter what the cost!"

As he said the words, Maggie's sharp mind raced back to Alfred; to his insistence that Danegeld would no longer be paid.

"Eurogeld!" she blurted, slamming her fist on the table. "Eurogeld!"

Instantly she stopped herself, aware she had momentarily been unable to contain her frustration. But rescue came from Urquart, the senior civil servant who had backed her earlier.

"If I may interject," he asked with immaculate manners. The room looked away from Maggie and back to him. He spoke softly but with great conviction giving firepower to his words.

"Maggie raises points that the rest of us shy away from. We must ask ourselves one crucial question above all others." He paused. The room fell silent all eyes upon him. "Who are we here to serve? The Government or the people? For some may say at the end of this we failed in our duty! Our fault is that we should have mobilised behind either Canada or a World Trade Organisation strategy from the start and forced the EU's hand. If we had done so, then Brexit would have been delivered and the people's wishes respected. Downing Street's promises to take back control of our laws, our borders and our money would have been kept."

Sir Stephen Dawkins glared at him unable to accept these words coming from such a senior member of the Civil Service. Sentiments such as these he could just about stomach from Maggie but from Urquart such comments amounted almost to insurrection. Downing Street would be obeyed. By far the majority of his colleagues around the table in this august institution, the Civil Service that had overseen the transfer from Empire to Commonwealth and done the Government's bidding in peace and in war would not be found wanting he said.

The PM knew best; Downing Street and the Cabinet knew best – the people most assuredly did not and that was all there was to it.

Chapter 7

Summer 2018

Onslow Ratcliffe sat alone in his office. It was a pleasant enough room, smaller than he would like but made attractive by a window affording views across the gardens below to the Thames beyond. The weather in London had broken some days ago and the highest temperatures since the great summer of '76 seemed now in the distant past. Nevertheless he pulled at his tie and loosened his top button. He leant back in his chair and crossed his feet upon the red leather bound desk: his elder colleagues would not approve but he cared not. There was a touch of the arrogance of youth about him.

His half drunk coffee was now cold. Beside it on the desk lay various files all marked 'Confidential', their contents known only to him and a selected few of his Brexit negotiating colleagues. The papers inside were dynamite. If they had got into the wrong hands all hell would have been let loose. Downing Street would have gone berserk if the revelations had gone public. At their core were their revised negotiating entry positions regarding several key issues. Each one was actually below the bottom lines that had been earlier spelt out and repeated interminably by the Prime Minister. The most basic laws of negotiation had been broken and lay in tatters he knew. Yet his mind was consumed upon his task: Britain's closeness to Europe was all that mattered. Besides, so long as those files remained in his safe keeping who would ever know?

His thoughts flickered like a butterfly not knowing where to settle, between the meeting, Maggie's remarks and their last date together. And then there was Ingrid. She had lingered in his mind and now armed with Sir Stephen's blessing to use his Brussels contacts he would see her again. Francois' words flashed back to him: his oddly enigmatic description of her role. He slipped his hand into his pocket and pulled out the card she had been so keen to give him. He dialled the number and waited but there was no answer. He left a message for her to call him, confident she would do so. He did not have long to wait.

"Onslow," she said. "Is that you?"

Her voice was expressive, enhanced by her sexy accent that had made its mark upon him before.

"Ingrid, how are you?" he asked.

"I am fine thank you, just fine. Are you coming to Brussels soon, Onslow?"

"I would like to come over later this week. Would you be free to meet Ingrid, on Thursday or Friday?"

Her response came quickly. She mirrored his directness. "I should like that very much. Shall we say Thursday at six at the bar we met at last time near the Commission?" Her words came keenly, but constrained and confident, as if there were a certain formality to these things, borne Onslow thought, from the refined European culture he had witnessed during his times in Brussels.

"I will look forward to seeing you Ingrid. Good bye."

Onslow Ratcliffe put the phone down. He began to pace. He paused at the window and took in the view. A smile spread across his lips.

Three miles away Maggie had arrived back at her flat in Kensington. She had stopped at Harrods and taken her time selecting particular delicacies from the food hall. She had earned a treat she told herself.

The flat looked tidy as it always did. She had saved hard to buy it four years previously, made possible only by a combination of her generous salary and like others from fortunate backgrounds, the bank of Mum and Dad. She felt for the millions unable to even consider a property purchase. Unlike some of her colleagues, she had welcomed Osborne's tax changes designed to put more of the housing stock into the hands of young prospective owner occupiers rather than to rapacious landlords.

Her parents' generation had had it good she felt passionately. The multiples of earnings to property values had changed hugely since their day, particularly in London. Not only that but the impact of university fees had made their mark. Now her strong social conscience told her it was time for change. Yet in her view it was the Government that needed to change its policies – on these issues quite apart from Brexit. If it failed to do so then the thought of a hard left Labour Government filled her with foreboding. She had read the internal reports of what the consequences would be, attractive as it was to many of her generation who knew nothing of the seventies and eighties. High taxes, high spending and high borrowing were not a panacea as some of her friends believed them to be: more a recipe for economic disaster, she knew.

She took a shower and put on some old clothes. How strange it was she thought that the clothes she chose made such a difference to her well being. She opened the fridge and poured herself a glass of Sauvignon Blanc and for several moments did nothing more than stare out of the window, her glass in her hand. Outside the light was beginning to fade. The rush hour had passed its worst and Kensington Church Street took on a less busy air.

When the phone rang she felt in no hurry to answer. It was Onslow.

"Maggie, how are you?" he enquired. She hadn't seen him since their tense meeting at work several days ago. Neither had she spoken to him by phone following their open disagreement. Yet still she determined to keep their relationship on track.

"I'm fine. I didn't see you in Whitehall today. How are you?" she asked him.

"Oh, I've been busy. I'm sorry I did not call you." His words were concise making no effort to elaborate. She wondered whether he would refer to their meeting, but like her he preferred to give it no mention.

"Maggie," he continued, "I'm going to be away for a few days. I have to go back to Brussels so cannot see you this week. I'll call you at the weekend when I'm back."

When she put down the phone she turned again to the window and drank from her glass holding the fresh cool wine on her palate before swallowing. Her perspicacious mind ran over Onslow's words and tone. He was going again to Brussels to follow through the actions agreed at their meeting, but maybe there was more to it, she deduced. Perhaps she was wrong, but she would not dwell on it.

75

She picked up the newspaper that lay unread upon the coffee table and turned the page spotting a small headline seemingly of little significance. Her eye darted over the text. Brussels the report said was spending nearly a million pounds upon buying 751 new television sets, one for every MEP, including the British contingent.

How strange she thought. We were supposed to be leaving. The extravagance she had witnessed at first hand bore no surprise to her. In the scheme of things it was a trifling sum. Yet her mind raced back to her discussions in Whitehall. They needed our money she thought more than her colleagues appreciated and we appeared only too willing to give it.

She let the thought subside. She would focus instead upon the Harrods delicacies. As she walked to the little kitchen however, the phone rang again. It was Stella enquiring about meeting up. The thought brought an instant smile to her face.

"Stella," she said. "Let's meet later this week. Onslow has to go to Brussels again. You can show me your photos of Monpazier and Sarlat. Besides, I'd like to talk to you." There was a pause at the other end as Stella registered her words.

"Are you alright, Maggie?" she asked. "You sound as if something's on your mind."

Maggie hesitated before answering. "Yes," she said. "Let's talk then, I'll look forward to it." She had hidden her frustration. They agreed a time.

She sat back on the sofa, her mind once again reverting to her role within the Brexit negotiations. Stella she knew would once more be a welcome distraction. But there seemed no way to hide it. She felt an overwhelming feeling of despondency. No longer could she deny that what she was now witnessing was nothing less than a humiliation, a dishonest humiliation at that. Not only that but she was an accessory to the crime. Instead of defiance she witnessed conciliation; instead of integrity she witnessed dishonesty and instead of a vision for freedom she witnessed only a willingness to succumb to eternal vassalage.

In stark contrast her thoughts switched to Alfred and his defiance from Somerset. Did not the principled Member of Parliament leading the European Research Group also represent Somerset? How strange she thought: but then this was only one of many points of comparison she had astutely noted as she read of Alfred. She wondered what he would do next and opened her book looking for inspiration.

April – May 878

From the moment he had arrived at Athelney on the eve of Easter the 23rd March, 878 after being on the run since the first week of the New Year, Alfred had been determined to keep alive more than a mere ray of hope. Immediately he had sent out trusted messengers along the Roman roads and tracks dating back into antiquity. Their objective he commanded them was to get word to the aldermen and reeves in the shires that he, Alfred was alive and that the fight back would commence in the spring. He was aware of the risks for no word of his whereabouts must reach Guthrum. The danger he knew was that if all hope had been allowed to be lost then the temptation to parley and collude with the Vikings would have been all the greater. There were defeatists around him, many who in their own self interest would give up the fight and accept the Viking stranglehold.

Indeed he suspected some of already having done so, even members of his own family based at Wimborne. As history so often taught, it was the establishment, the wealthy land-owners who would do whatever it took to protect their position. If he could not secure a major victory then very possibly the thegns and aldermen would turn against him and sue for peace. Conciliation and concession, the very things he had resisted so strongly would become the order of the day.

Alfred had risen early. He looked down at his beautiful Ellie who lay still asleep: the cock crowed signalling that dawn had broken. He crept out of their shelter careful not to wake her. Several of his men were already up and they saw him approaching.

The time was coming shortly he told them. Soon would be the moment when they would make their move. Alfred knew he had the advantage of a communication network that formed their sophisticated Anglo-Saxon system of administration. Each of the shires overseen by their reeve, the local thegn and aldermen had their own assembly points – the military hubs mobilising the fyrds, the local militia: thankfully the Viking incursions had failed to break their intricate network.

As the morning sun rose he sat with those who had acted as the messengers of hope just weeks before. He ordered them to return again to the shires, to the assembly points in Somerset, Wiltshire and Hampshire. There they were to summon the local fighting men to rendezvous at Whitsun, the day upon which the Holy Spirit had descended upon the disciples at Pentecost. It lay in the seventh week after Easter – the first week of May – and would be understood by all who heard his message. Their rallying point would be at Egbert's Stone at the eastern edge of Selwood Forest.

The place lay on the western rim of Salisbury Plain, a little south of Warminster. Egbert's Stone commemorating his respected grandfather was significant to the men of Wessex. Alfred could think of nowhere better.

Yet he was not confident the call would be answered. Several months had passed since they had been together united as one. If the call went unheeded by the reeves and aldermen all would be lost. Throughout that day whenever Ellie looked at him she noticed his demeanour. As ever he had tried to hide it from her, assuming a look of confidence. But she knew him too well. She could read Alfred – his changes of mood, his vulnerabilities, his passion for the cause – and anyway she wanted only to support him. That night as they fell asleep in each other's arms she held him tightly trying to read his thoughts.

"They will come Alfred, they will answer your call. Sleep my love, sleep my love," she whispered to him. He stroked her skin and kissed her. His mind was restless but her words gave him comfort. Every leader needed a strong partner he thought as sleep overcame him.

The following days passed without incident. Every preparation for their advance was made. Guthrum had halted at Chippenham, the spies reported to Alfred. His Great Army had foregone the chase perhaps frustrated Alfred believed by the defeat of Ubba and his army in Devon. Perhaps the tectonic plates of war were moving in his favour he mused, but all depended upon the rally of his forces at Egbert's Stone. He had known the area since his boyhood. If he could marshal sufficient numbers then already he had determined where he might join battle but much could change between now and Whitsun.

Unknown to Alfred however, his trusty messengers had been diligent. Across the three shires they had ridden hard between each of the assembly points passing their sovereign's message just as he had commanded. Alfred had deliberately avoided sending them to Devon and Dorset. Ubba and his great Viking army may have been defeated but he was acutely aware of Guthrum's propensity for a two pronged attack. The risk of another seaborne invasion remained high: fighting men needed to remain stationed at the coast.

But in respect of Dorset there was another reason also for him to keep his plans from them. His suspicions remained that some, especially the aldermen and nobility had already been suborned by Guthrum with the promise to repay their allegiance. Many times Alfred had sat at his camp fire trying to get inside the mind of Guthrum: if the Viking leader could stretch his tentacles over time, normalising life but under his ultimate authority then the vassalage of Wessex would have been achieved. Yet the defeat of Alfred would speed matters considerably!

As his messengers rode, demanding the presence of those loyal to him at Egbert's Stone that Whitsun, men across the three shires heard the call.

A youth barely into his teens named Osbert listened to the rider who brought the news from the reeve at Wilton. As the messenger galloped on, he ran into his parents' arms and demanded they let him go. His mother cried uncontrollably knowing full well it would probably be the last time she ever saw her son. She cried all the more when her husband not yet too old to wield an axe insisted upon accompanying the boy. They cried in each other's arms and embraced a final time. Then armed with spear and axe they began their intrepid walk following the old trails past the farms and fields that had been so familiar to them.

All across the shires the call was answered: fathers, husbands, sons and brothers rousing themselves to action walking as fast as they could through wet fields and muddied brooks brought on by the spring rains. They walked together sharing jokes to keep their spirits up, each giving comfort to the other knowing that their cause was just. Others from their locality joined them, some of whom they recognised as they met together at the thegn. They made anxious companions but their belief that under Alfred there was at least a chance of throwing off the Viking yoke gave hope.

The more fortunate rode their horses. A few were equipped with armour and the trappings of wealth. For the most part however, their weapons were old; the family sword passed down through the generations, the rusty dagger used till now for household purposes, and the spear kept sharp for killing animals not men. They carried their sacks too, containing food to give them sustenance for the journey. As they met with others they shared the latest news. Alfred was alive they had heard, but could it really be true? Their inspirational leader who had led them both in pursuit and in retreat of the Viking armies, could he really be alive, they asked?

Onwards they went along ancient tracks, fording the streams, along valleys replete with the freshness of spring growth, seeing new leaves upon the trees beneath which rabbits scampered and deer roamed. The tryst at Whitsun was symbolic too. The God of love planting his spirit upon the disciples who, armed with unstoppable power would then go out to tell the world the Good News. Was this not an

81

augur for them too? Was God not bringing his hand of providence to bear upon them also?

As they journeyed on they buoyed their spirits with bawdy humour telling stories, forging new friendships made easy by the sharing of a common cause. If battle was indeed to be joined many of them would die they knew. But many would live too if they could win the victory and all Wessex would be rid of the Viking curse. The belief that the messages from their king were not falsely put about rumours, but might actually be true was what motivated them. And more news now arrived which spurred them on. Alfred was on the move they were told. Alfred was on the move!

Before long the sight of burning beacons on the hilltops met their eyes, the rallying points and camp sites set up by the aldermen across the shires readying them for their march to Selwood. The beacon fires were symbolic to those brave men, signifying as at other times in their island's story that some great happening, uniting them in common cause, was afoot. Onward they went as dawn broke the next day; onward to their destination not knowing whether Alfred would be there. But Alfred was there and when they saw him riding towards them, emerging from the shady trees of Selwood Forest they were overjoyed. He had discarded his disguise. Now he rode majestically in full regalia with etchings of gold and garnets, wearing armour breastplate and holding a banner aloft. Strong men cried as they saw him. For a brief moment many stopped, unable to accept this was actually him, wondering whether it was an illusion, a ghost of their former Alfred they had loved and followed. But no, it was truly him.

Other armed groups were now making their way forward.

Ellie raised her hand shielding her eyes from the low sun as afternoon gave way to dusk. She had spotted the weary bands of men carrying their weapons, moving inexorably towards them.

"Look Alfred, look yonder," she cried. "More are coming, many more!"

Alfred saw them as Edgar his trusted warrior came and stood by him. "Sire, your call has been answered. May God be praised," he cried.

"Indeed Edgar, indeed. But give me more Oh Lord, give me more!" he replied.

Ellie hugged this man she loved. She grinned from ear to ear as she watched the men gathering, many coming forward to Alfred unable to restrain their joy. The sound of men's voices, a magical mixture of merriment and relief, filled the air. Alfred turned to her and spoke above the din, but no one but she heard his happy words. She smiled and squeezed his arm. "Your dream Alfred, everything you have strived so hard for, this is your reward."

He smiled but said nothing. His brain was still swirling, restive for more scores of good hearted men to even up the odds with Guthrum. But he did not have long to wait. He looked across the fields again. More bands were making their weary way towards them from west Wiltshire. Soon they were joined by men from Hampshire and soon after by those from Somerset who had followed from the west in their leader's footsteps. He had noticed however, that no men from Dorset had arrived.

"Those men who have not answered my call and who have colluded with the Vikings should hang their heads in shame. These vipers will stand accursed this day," Alfred exclaimed.

Rarely had Ellie heard him excoriate other Anglo-Saxons this way. But the Whitsun weekend was not over and as dawn broke the next morning more bands of men arrived, this time from the east.

Alfred stood amongst them exchanging hearty words inspiring each man with confidence in his destiny. The battle would be taken to the Vikings he told them. They would fight and not concede. They would turn their defiance into leverage so strong they would force the issue in their favour and negotiate the peace from strength. Ellie watched as bedraggled men some mere boys, others who had fought before, now raised themselves to their full height, their confidence and pride at the prospect of securing for themselves the status of a sovereign people now restored; the prospect of freedom within their grasp.

Alfred stood now on a ledge and looked out upon his little army. He held his arms aloft and as he did so the sounds of birds in the trees were drowned by cheers. Standing erect his sword out of its sheath, he addressed the gathering:

"On this Whitsun day destiny has commanded that we do our duty. All of us have lived for this moment, for today my friends is when we turn our vision and our defiance into glorious victory. Be in no doubt my friends we have it in our hearts to do the deed – and do the deed we will.

You ask what is our cause? I can tell you in one word. Freedom. Freedom for all our people. For surely in God's name we deserve nothing less. Freedom, to make our own laws, freedom to control our own borders, freedom for every man to work his plough and provide for his loved ones without hindrance.

You ask who are we fighting for? I will tell you my friends. For every sweet man among us. For our sweet women, for our sweet children. Yes for our children. For our children's children. For our children's children's children. Freedom for all our future generations so that in a thousand years those in our blood strain will still remember our deeds and tell their children ...they did it for us. Therefore, let no man concede in fright. Let no man betray our cause. Let no man collude with the enemy or give him succour. For if he should undermine us then as God is my witness, he shall himself be damned in eternal hell."

Alfred gestured as his voice grew louder, quickening and soaring at times into a roaring crescendo. Not a single man took his eyes off him as they stood entranced and mesmerised by his oratory.

"So let us rouse ourselves and stir our souls, for my friends have we been cowering like frightened children these last few months, frightened into obeyance and subjugation? No, I tell you thrice No! Have we not my friends, every man amongst us, have we not instead prepared ourselves like our fine horses straining upon the start, like greyhounds in the slip, like caged and ferocious boars ready to hurl ourselves upon the enemy?"

A mighty roar arose at these words. The emotion of what was at stake was almost palpable.

All Alfred's brave men; men from humble dwellings who had picked up their axes and rallied to him, all gave cheer, their eyes upon him, their fists punching the air in salute as his words struck home.

"Our blood is up. God is with us. Our cause is noble for surely there can be no nobler cause than this. Let us therefore brace ourselves to do our duty for without freedom all England will sink into the dark abyss, subdued and defiled under foreign hands, pitiful, shamed and unforgiven by future generations."

Ellie looked up at Alfred. As his oratory soared, the tears flowed down her cheeks. But these were not tears of sorrow, not tears of foreboding no, these were tears of joy brought on by his rhetoric; joy that today was the start of a new dawn in which their freedom might at last be won. Defiance would now be turned into victory. If there had been any who questioned Alfred's leadership, from that moment on his leadership was in no doubt. The defeatists had been defeated.

Cicero had written that the peroration of any speech should reach the emotions and inspire its listeners. Alfred had done precisely that. Everyone who heard him that Whitsun morning knew in his heart his words would not be empty but that very day be turned into action.

Summer 2018

Maggie put down the book. Tears were pouring down her cheeks also, she realised.

Chapter 8

Autumn 2018

The phone had not rung all morning and Maggie had enjoyed a productive period shut away in her quiet Whitehall office. She sat concentrating hard upon papers that required her total attention when suddenly the silence was broken like a laser beam cutting through her thoughts. She sighed and picked up the phone.

"Maggie, Crispin Urquart here, how are you?"

She hesitated, just a little startled. She could never remember taking a call from him before.

"I'm fine, thank you," she replied. "What can I do for you?"

"I've been having serious thoughts following our recent meeting concerning Chequers, you remember?" His voice sounded controlled but anxious, guarded in his language.

"Yes, of course."

"Well, I think it might be wise for us to meet together. How are you fixed for lunch today?"

Maggie noted his choice of words. Momentarily she felt bewildered but quickly composed herself.

"That would be fine Crispin. Where do you suggest?"

"Well, I think it best we meet somewhere away from the

office. Shall we say 1.00 at Gino's on the South Bank, you know, near the Festival Hall?"

"Yes, okay. I'll be there," she replied.

She put the phone down and sat quite still in contemplation. Whatever it was he needed to speak to her about, it sounded intriguing. Her mind flashed back to their meeting three days ago. Urquart's words of support had impressed her, unlike those of Onslow whose insistence upon going back to Brussels had confirmed her suspicions of progressing with as she saw it, the Chequers cover up.

She held up the picture she had framed and placed neatly in front of her. It was of the square at Domme where she and Stella had stopped on their last day in the Dordogne. She remembered it well. The stunning bastide fortified town perched high over the river almost but not entirely impregnable. Only a short time had passed but it seemed longer. She had spoken to Stella again. Instead of meeting as they had planned, Stella had decided to throw a dinner party and with Onslow away she was looking forward to it.

She closed the office door behind her and walked from the building. In a few minutes she had strode passed the assorted anti terrorist barriers on Westminster Bridge and found herself below the London Eye. How ugly those barriers were she thought: how sad that London should be defaced by the threat of terrorist violence. She stopped for a moment and stared at the top of the Eye. Any movement was barely discernible. She had not been up it despite having lived in London for years. Somehow it had not appealed and besides it would me nothing compared to the views in the Dordogne she conjectured.

The walk beside the river felt good. A light breeze and a

clear sky was conducive to clear thinking yet by the time she had reached Gino's she had still not guessed Urquart's intent. He was already there and beckoned her to the table in the corner. He was dressed as she had noticed him before. The same suit she was sure; definitely the same expensive grey tie. His black Oxford shoes were well polished she noticed. She liked what she saw but there was no sexual attraction, only a respect for this nicely dressed middle aged individual. As they sat she observed the urbane figure of Crispin Urquart more closely; his sallow complexion, his receding hairline but well cut hair. His teeth were uncommonly white she observed and his smile was beguiling. He was not unattractive.

They ordered pasta dishes on to which Urquart poured lashings of parmesan cheese, something she couldn't abide. Over a carafe of red wine she waited for him to enlighten her.

"Thank you for joining me. Sorry it was at such short notice," he said politely. He sipped his wine, thinking how best to get to the point.

"May I ask how you felt about the meeting the other day?"

Maggie thought for a few seconds uncertain to what extent she should unveil her true reflections. She remained guarded at first, reticent to say too much.

"I was frustrated," she said. "Perhaps I said more than I should."

He smiled a look of reassurance. "No you did not, let me reassure you. At least not too much as far as I was concerned." This last caveat struck Maggie. She wondered what he was driving at.

"Maggie," he went on. "Your views upon the cover up for

Chequers are exactly in line with my own feelings. That term cover up. I hope it does not offend you?"

She felt herself relax. If he had used the term then she was at liberty too.

"Not at all. That is what we discussed after all."

"Quite so, quite so." Urquart sipped his wine giving himself time to choose his words carefully. "The thing is, how can I put this? We have to be careful how we make our views known."

"What do you mean Crispin?" It was the first occasion she had addressed him by his Christian name.

"I wanted to warn you."

"Warn me! Warn me about what?" she interjected.

"Warn you, perhaps advise you that our comments are being carefully monitored and noted." Urquart paused to register her reaction but she showed none, preferring to let him talk on. She said nothing.

"You see if you or I are seen to be rocking the boat then that will not go down well. To put it bluntly, our careers could be affected."

His revelation came as little surprise. Nevertheless a look of disgust came over her face which she was unable to hide.

"Our careers?" she pressed him.

"Our careers," Urquart reiterated calmly. "You see Maggie, Downing Street does not take kindly to those of us who have the temerity to reveal what is going on! And our masters at the most senior level are not amused either. They will stick to the Downing Street line whatever."

Now it was Maggie who swigged from her glass. Still she said nothing.

"There is more I'm afraid which I feel compelled to share

with you. Our detractors who as you saw are many, could how shall I say, choose to make life difficult for us. If even the suggestion arose that we might spill the beans to a baying mob of journalists for instance, they would have us for breakfast as the saying goes. They will do anything to silence us!"

Maggie interrupted his flow.

"What do you mean Crispin, in what way?"

"They could if they wished accuse us each of being in breach of the Official Secrets Act, the penalties for which I do not need to underline to you. I know it sounds appalling when all we are doing is seeking to carry out the people's will, but there it is."

For several seconds Maggie was silent.

"Then what are you suggesting? Should we reveal what we know if Downing Street persists with Chequers? And if so how do we let the cat out of the bag about the violation of red lines and the disguise Onslow is seeking with the help of the EU?"

"Through leaking not to the press Maggie, but to members of Parliament, just a few select members you understand. As you know they have the privilege of being able to say anything without retribution. Remember how the good name of Leon Brittan was traduced by a Labour figure under parliamentary privilege? The poor man was innocent and died without knowing his name had been cleared. It was a travesty."

Urquart paused and leant back in his chair. Maggie thought back to her study of history and was instantly reminded of the lessons of the thirties.

"Didn't the brave Tory rebels gain their information about

Chamberlain's appeasement and the real situation from civil servant leaks?" she asked him.

"They did indeed. You know your history," he replied. "And then too, almighty pressure was put upon everyone to support the PM. Nothing has changed Maggie, nothing has changed."

"So are you going to talk to MPs?" she asked.

"Not yet. We must wait till the moment is right. We must hold our fire. But let's stay in close touch. We must be careful, do you understand?"

Maggie had heard enough. They walked together back towards Westminster Bridge. He spoke of lighter matters but she barely heard him. Urquart's comments reverberated in her mind. Half way across they paused and leant against the wall and gazed down upon the Thames. She looked at the great Palace of Westminster to their right, the gentle green grey waters lapping at its terrace. She turned to face him.

"Crispin," she asked. "Have you ever read the story of Alfred the Great, his darkest hour?"

"I can't say I have, why do you ask?" Urquart sounded intrigued.

"I am reading, studying from a wonderful book based upon the Anglo-Saxon Chronicle. His vision, his defiance, his leadership, there are so many things he did to win back our freedom that our own leadership could learn from."

Urquart smiled. "You sound like a romantic Maggie."

"Maybe, but I have counted scores of acts of leadership that Downing Street could have emulated. It could all have been handled so differently. Have we learned nothing from history?"

"I should like to read this book of yours. May be we can

use it to pass some lessons to our masters, but I doubt they will listen."

"Downing Street is not exactly known to listen," she said wryly.

Crispin Urquart reached inside his pocket and took out the black Cartier fountain pen he always carried and a tiny notepad. Maggie had seen the tiny notepad Wellington used to give his commands when she had visited Wellington Arch. Perhaps Urquart could use his to similar effect. She instantly dismissed the notion. He asked her for the title of her book and he carefully wrote it down.

"My bedtime reading, thank you!" he joked. But Maggie knew what they were about was no laughing matter.

* * *

The upper floors of the offices of the European Commission were reserved for the more senior bureaucrats. They had been beautifully designed with every attention to detail without regard to cost. Their coffers were big and anyway the auditors had not passed the accounts for many a year. Keeping them up to the sumptuous requirements of their occupiers who controlled the purse strings had been taken for granted.

A secretary smartly dressed in red, walked swiftly rather than hurriedly along the marble corridor. Her bearing was upright and business like. In her hands she held a silver bottomed tray upon which lay a jug of freshly ground coffee. A bowl of finest Belgian chocolates was placed neatly between two elegantly designed cups and saucers. As she reached the end of the corridor the noise of her brisk steps from her high heels disappeared. She had reached the richly carpeted area that announced this was the inner sanctum of power. She knocked twice upon the imposing door and poked her head around.

Inside the enormous lounge euphemistically referred to as an office, four cream leather sofas formed a square around a marble coffee table upon which stood an elegant glass bowl containing a display of freshly cut orchids in a myriad of colours. The walls were pure white, broken at intervals down one side by precisely placed paintings of abstract nature each competing to make their statement. On the opposite wall a large television had been carefully placed. Various alcoholic beverages and several cut crystal glasses lay haphazardly upon a glass table. At the back of the room a huge plate glass window afforded one of the finest views over Brussels. Seated in a high back chair in cream nappa leather, Francois Du Bain beckoned her forward: she placed the tray upon the oversized desk that stretched before him.

"Thank you my dear," he said. She smiled first to him and then to his visitor who sat opposite him quietly, and left the room. Francois poured out two coffees and passed one to Ingrid. "I think you like it black," he said. She returned his smile and sipped from the cup.

The chemistry between them was warm and friendly. Frequently they had drank together outside of work but always on a platonic basis. As when Francois had taken Ingrid and Onslow to his club and plied them both with champagne he had always been generous to her. She after all was a highly useful member of his Brexit negotiating team.

"Ingrid, you are meeting Onslow at 6.0 is that right?" he asked.

"Yes, at the usual place." The thought of seeing Onslow Ratcliffe again had excited her. True, she hardly knew him and even her perceptive first impressions might be wrong. Yet she had convinced herself the evening would be both pleasurable and worthwhile.

Francois leant forward in his chair and began to speak earnestly.

"Let's go over again your objectives Ingrid. The British have not negotiated well up to now but even so we should not underestimate them. They are telling us they have no room to move on Chequers but we are sure they do. Their own Chancellor has signalled how desperate they are for a deal after all. Their Treasury have helped our cause immeasurably."

A smile of satisfaction spread across his lips. "Their Parliament in both Houses are also desperate for a deal – either that or a second referendum as their Remainers keep telling me. I think we can assume they will give us everything we demand." He sat back in his chair and grinned again before continuing.

"Yes, the visits from our informers, those wonderful British 'Vichy' collaborators, have been so helpful to us. I think that after this is over I will present them each with a special medal for their loyalty to the European project. We will put them on a podium and play 'Ode to Joy' Ingrid don't you think?" He sank back in his huge high backed chair and clapped his hands together, an equally huge smile across his face. Ingrid mirrored his obvious pleasure at the remark unsure of whether her chief was joking, though she shared the sentiment.

"I want you to make it clear to him that we will not give

ground Ingrid. We expect Britain to pay the price. You and I know the British must be seen by others to be punished. You are to manage Onslow's expectations Ingrid, making it clear they must concede more to our demands or they will have no deal."

"I understand Francois. I will make it clear I promise you."

"I know you will, my dear. But do not forget your other goals for your meeting this evening. Please reinforce that the common rule book must mean total compliance with the EU's technical regulations, nothing less. The UK will not be allowed to make itself more competitive. It's all about managing their expectations Ingrid; they must know there is no alternative."

She nodded, but Francois hadn't finished yet.

"It will be helpful to know their real bottom line on immigration in so far as preferential treatment for EU citizens is concerned." He paused and smiled. "I know you have your ways and means, my dear. You can get more out of this man in one night than we can ever hope to in our formal negotiations."

Ingrid understood his meaning. It was not the first time she had used her female charms to uphold the European project.

"I want you also to find out their actual bottom line regarding British judges paying due regard to the European Court of Justice. Will they accept this means complete acceptance of the ECJ without question? Persuade him in whatever way you have to and find out their real bottom lines for me, would you? We have conceded almost nothing so far, I so prefer it that way!"

Francois touched her arm as if to emphasise the

importance he attached to her task. He reached inside a drawer and took out an envelope. "Ply him with champagne Ingrid and seduce him with your charms. Here is plenty of cash for your expenses tonight. Spend whatever you need. Take him wherever you want."

She took the envelope from him. She glanced inside noting the thick wad of 50 Euro notes.

"I will not let you down Francois. I shall report back to you tomorrow."

They stood and embraced one another. He held her by the arms and kissed her on both cheeks rather as a loving uncle might. Then he ran his fingers through his greasy hair with a look of satisfaction upon his face.

"Have a pleasurable evening!" he whispered in her ear.

Chapter 9

Autumn 2018

Onslow Ratcliffe had arrived earlier than he expected at the square in the centre of Brussels in which his assignation with Ingrid was planned. He glanced at his watch noting a half hour to go. He strolled nonchalantly towards the Grand Place and looked up at the architecture. Unlike Maggie his knowledge of history was limited. Yet he knew enough to set his imagination stirring: German troops taking over the place in a trice after their lightning strike and Belgium's instant capitulation: how they would have strutted across this beautiful square asserting their supremacy, their machine guns and armoured cars on overt display. He thought of the First World War and tried to imagine similar scenes. Wellington too flashed through his mind as he had won the victory at Waterloo not many miles south.

But Onslow's mind kept returning to the job in hand. He reminded himself of his main task; he recalled the words of Sir Stephen telling him to get the job done, to concede if necessary but above all to win agreement that the EU would disguise the full extent of the British concessions. Downing Street depended upon it. Indeed the very future of the Prime Minister could depend upon it.

He glanced again at his watch. It was nearly 6.0 and he walked more briskly this time back to the little bar. Ingrid was not there he noticed. He took advantage and selected a table where they could talk unheard by others. He remembered the last time he had been here, Francois telling him how this was a frequent haunt of the EU apparatchiks. He remembered too Francois' strange words describing Ingrid's role, aware that her influence with her boss could be decisive. He recalled how keen she had been for him to accept her card, pressing it into his hand. Somehow she had seemed almost overly keen he reminisced – or was it simply his innate sexual attraction that had motivated her? He chose to imagine the latter, yet the attraction was entirely mutual and since their meeting he had imagined her in his arms on more than one occasion.

He pulled at his cuffs displaying his cufflinks, then at his tie preening himself in preparation for their tryst. Deliberately he had worn his smartest suit, and an expensive shirt he had purchased as always from Jermyn Street. He had taken care with his tie knot: indeed it had become almost a compulsive obsession as he had noted the difference between those of Trump and Obama. There was just a touch of vanity to his character but a vanity entirely in keeping with his suave smugness and the rakish charm he could turn on at will. That charm had won Maggie to him just months before, but now it was his other traits that weighed with her more.

"Onslow, there you are." Instantly he turned as he recognised Ingrid's sexy voice with her accent that had so entranced him before. He stood immediately and embraced her. She kissed him upon both his cheeks before drawing back and looking at him admiringly. "You look good

Onslow. It is so nice to see you." She touched his forearms as the words came from her lips.

They sat opposite each other across the little table. The air was still warm and a shaft of sunlight was upon her face. Her skin looked as fresh and sun kissed as before; her high cheek bones and gorgeous face made up with just a hint of make up; her mouth perfectly formed and inviting to any man who cast his eye upon her. She wore the merest touch of lipstick. She was no tart he knew: Ingrid was a highly sophisticated and refined young lady and intelligent with it. A self confidence he found alluring exuded from her like her perfume – attractive, seductive even to those she intended.

"What would you like to drink?" he asked her.

"She again placed her hand on his arm and spoke never taking her eyes off his.

"No Onslow, tonight is on me, I insist. After all you are a guest in my city." She smiled giving him no option other than to accept her offer. "Shall we begin with a cold glass of fine white? The evening is yet young!"

She selected a bottle. "Do you love fine wine Onslow? I am very selective." She paused, then continued: "A little like I am with most things!"

She let her hand rest upon his for a moment. "Anyway I guess we should talk about our business, about the negotiations don't you think – before we can talk about other things," she added.

As they chatted, her ability to switch from one moment being subtly flirtatious to the next being business like and direct confounded Onslow Ratcliffe. The sexual frisson between them was tangible: he knew he was being led by this master practitioner in whatever direction she intended but was unable to do anything other than respond. Only temporarily when the waiter took the bottle from their ice bucket and poured them each another glass did he feel the spell lifting only then to be dashed as she again took control.

"Onslow we need dinner, we need food don't you think?" she asked. There was something, some subliminal message in her suggestion contained within her choice of words that evaded Onslow. "Shall we dine here, but if you prefer we can go to a little place I know around the corner? The food is the best in Brussels I am sure. It is very, how shall I say, intimate, but you don't mind that do you Onslow?"

He smiled at her holding her stare. "Of course not, that would be nice," he answered.

She pressed more than enough money into the waiter's hand and did not wait for change. Onslow watched as she rose from her seat. She was as elegant and expensively dressed as previously. She wore a black, loose fitting dress which as she walked revealed tantalising glimpses of her legs. They were tanned and perfectly toned he noticed. She slung an arm around his waist and led him out of the square, their hips moving side by side as if two ballroom dancers moving together in perfect harmony.

The little restaurant exuded a romantic air, its lights low with hanging baskets draping fragrant flowers between the tables. The stone walls looked old, deliberately left untouched displaying evidence of its history. The romances, the secret assignations, the conspirators and the financial dealers; Onslow wondered what secrets lay hidden within these walls? The waiter showed them to the table Ingrid had selected earlier. They sat closely together and when she suggested champagne he consented. A lit candle had been placed strategically between them.

The food they ordered was exquisite, not in quantity which was slight but tantalising to their taste buds. As they talked she sought the answers and information Francois had requested. Whenever he obliged she smiled seductively suggestive of his reward to come.

"You are good looking Onslow, you must know that," she remarked as she sipped from her glass, her steely blue eyes meeting his. "There is one more thing I would love you to confide in me before we can think of other things. The other sums beyond the £39 billion, the other sums the EU expects over the years ahead will be forthcoming won't they, to make our trading deal last of course?"

She let her hand glide over his as she waited for his answer. He glanced down. The light from the candle made her skin all the more seductive. He wanted to stroke her flesh, to make love to her.

"I cannot possibly say Ingrid, you will understand. But..." he hesitated.

"I understand of course, but..." she pressed him, her hand still resting upon his. She fixed him with her stare never blinking. She too had been taught the art of negotiation.

"But I am sure that will prove no problem," he conceded.

Ingrid sipped from her glass and smiled.

"My hotel is close by. We can go there for an evening night cap Onslow, if you would like to, that is?" She let her hand slide under the table and rest upon his thigh. "Oh, but there is one thing more I must say to you." Again she held him in suspense taking him to the Garden of Eden and then holding him back playing with him like a cat with a mouse.

"You know too we are greatly concerned about needing preferential treatment for our EU citizens to come to Britain. Some in your Party seem not to want this Onslow. Tell me please you will make certain this is granted. We so want to agree a successful trade deal together with you?"

Again she remained silent obliging him to agree. Once again Onslow Ratcliffe consented.

She settled the bill pressing a bundle of notes into the waiter's hand. They rose and she led him passed candle lit tables, not noticing couples enjoying their intimate surroundings and business men agreeing their deals.

Outside darkness had descended. She held his hand. "Come on," she said. "I want you to come with me. We will go to my hotel now. It's very close."

She was in control. She required no consent knowing that her objectives had been accomplished and that she was more than happy to enjoy the night with him. The chemistry ran between them like an electric current. She gripped his hand leading him the short walk.

Onslow looked up at the swanky hotel entrance. It was not one he had frequented but knew it to be the most expensive in Brussels. As she led him through the lobby, Ingrid left him for a second and spoke quickly to the receptionist. "Bring please to the penthouse suite, a bottle of cold champagne," she said quietly.

In the bright lights Onslow saw again what a beautiful woman she was. Thirty at most, her thick blonde hair cascaded to her shoulders. She held her head high, her shoulders straight and her back upright exuding a confidence that he found irresistible; confidence in her intellect, but confidence above all in her sexual presence.

They entered the lift alone. She pressed the button as if dictating the events, totally in control. Immediately the door closed she put one arm around his neck letting her nails dig into his flesh pulling his lips to hers. She kissed him passionately savouring the intimacy. Sensing his willingness she placed her other hand on his crotch and let her fingers stroke the material. Instantly she felt Onslow's hands slide down her body, out of his control surrendering to her demands. It was a lust fuelled by adrenaline borne from a toxic mixture of power and high living; two people brought together, cocooned at the heart of a political maelstrom at the mercy of serendipity.

Suddenly the lift doors opened. They composed themselves in an instant and she led him to her suite. Inside, the room was large and sumptuous dominated by a mirrored ceiling below which was the most enormous bed he had ever seen with cushions all in red. Ingrid pressed several buttons and discreet lighting around the room came to life as if to salute the lovers. There was a knock on the door.

As the waiter entered, Onslow slipped into the bathroom. He looked into the mirror and threw cold water on his face. Somehow it freshened him and he felt his mind temporarily coming back under his control and able to focus. His expectations of a deal had come face to face with reality, or was it a false reality designed to intimidate him, he knew not. But as he had listened to Ingrid he knew instinctively that only through more concessions would Chequers be accepted. He thought of Ingrid's words, her careful phrasing; her flirtation mixed to perfection like a perfect cocktail that he had been unable to resist. However, he had revealed far too much he knew; he had said things he should never have disclosed, shadowy bottom lines and the promise of fresh concessions, and he had done so unconditionally. Now before it was too late he reminded himself of his task.

She turned and looked at him as he walked back into the room, one hand upon her hip in the manner of a model.

"Ingrid," he said as he stood in front of her, "I have said more than I should to you this evening, but there is something I must ask of you?"

She held the champagne bottle provocatively in front of him. It was Taittinger, her favourite brand. He watched her fingers wrapped around the cork easing it slowly. Those painted nails had been scratching at his skin in the lift only seconds before he thought, but somehow he kept his mind focussed.

"I need your assurance that the EU will camouflage and disguise the concessions we make to you. They must be hidden in the small print and not allowed the oxygen of publicity for that could bring down our government, do you understand?"

She answered slowly, accentuating her words. "I would have to talk to Francois, Onslow. It is he that makes the final decision, but I am sure he will listen to me."

She grinned and kissed him tenderly on the lips. She looked up into his eyes. "If I do this, we will make love now?" Her words adorned with her sensual accent came more as a command than a question. Onslow nodded.

"Then we have a deal and I think we need to seal that deal, don't you my love?" Ingrid told him.

She forced the cork, guiding the exploding champagne into their glasses. Suddenly he sensed that she was again in charge. As they drank, she held the cold champagne in her mouth and kissed him passionately. Then she drew back and let the dress slip from her shoulders but only so far. She reached her arms around his neck and kissed him for a long time pressing her breasts against him.

Then she withdrew again and sat on the side of the bed. She signalled to Onslow to stand in front of her and slowly she unbuttoned his clothing letting her hands roam freely. He looked down watching her movements running his fingers through her hair. The pleasure she gave to him was something Onslow had not experienced before; not from Maggie, nor from any of his previous lovers. But she was in control and before long it was she who stood in front of him and disrobed, never taking her eyes of his. Her breasts were beautiful Onslow thought, her waist taut giving way to her hips and thighs all in perfect proportion. His hands reached for her and stroked her skin sending little pulses of pleasure through her body.

He stood facing her. They clung to each other now, feeling their naked bodies pressed hard together. Onslow Ratcliffe had imagined this moment from their first encounter but it was she Ingrid, who had made the play. It was she who had pressed her card so firmly into his palms; it was she who had taken control like a film director dictating the scenes.

They lay together on the bed. She reached for the champagne and poured a little on to her breasts. It ran in trickles down her body. He watched as she stroked her hands across her breasts feeling the cold wetness upon her skin.

"Kiss me, my love," she commanded him. He leant over her and licked the champagne moving his lips tenderly down her body causing her to moan. But soon those moans were turned to cries as she felt her body release itself drowning her in ecstasy.

She nuzzled her lips to his ear. "You are a good lover Mr Onslow Ratcliffe," she whispered. "Lie on your back now. This is how I like it," she told him.

She straddled him moving her hips slowly and provocatively into position before beginning to gyrate. All the time she looked down at him letting her blonde hair fall so that it touched his chest, every now and again leaning down and kissing him passionately. She watched the effect she was having upon him, tantalising him as she had all evening, determined to give him satisfaction. It was not only her pleasure that mattered to Ingrid. Unlike their negotiation this would be a win-win outcome, one that satisfied them both in equal measure, the culmination to their evening. This was the climax, the final movement of the symphony, the peroration to a speech, the final act which brought them the ultimate relief.

She moved slowly, so slowly, her head and hair now thrown back, her back arched. Onslow watched; her closed eyes, her head wavering from side to side, her expression of bliss oblivious to everything as she bathed in her sensations of pleasure. He had seen this before he knew. He had imagined this exact picture as he had been enraptured at the Albert Hall that night. His mind flashed back to the gorgeous pianist who had put her interpretation upon Grieg's concerto. He had seen all this before imagining it was Ingrid succumbing to the exquisiteness of her pleasure moving so slowly, so tenderly over him.

She looked down and whispered to him.

"Like fine wine, all the best things in life should be taken slowly, Onslow, don't you think?" But her words were lost on him.

Then without warning she sensed the end was near. She accelerated her movements writhing and contorting herself, wailing uncontrollably, her legs lifting herself above him as her convulsions took hold.

It was the first time Ingrid had lost control that evening and in the morning she would regain her elegant composure.

Chapter 10

Autumn 2018

That evening 230 miles from Brussels, Maggie Taylor sat in her flat deciding what to wear. She threw on a casual top and smart jeans. They would be entirely appropriate she considered for Stella's dinner party. Anyway it was good to be out of her work clothes. It had been a tiring day and she had been looking forward to this opportunity to socialise. Tonight would do her good; the chance to meet new friends and to see Stella. Her array of shoes made her uncertain which to select. Not for the first time the paradox of choice had presented itself.

As she dressed she turned on the television. Channel 4 news had started and was interviewing an economics expert who had the annoying habit of beginning every answer with the prefix 'So... '. She decided to switch to something else. She had become irritated anyway at their Brexit coverage considering the programme a touch too biased towards the Remainers. To be fair it was not the only programme to have annoyed her in such a way.

She switched to LBC. Nigel Farage had started his show inviting listeners to call him with their views on the latest Brexit developments and in particular the selling of

Chequers. Many times Maggie had been tempted to call the programme. What she could reveal would be dynamite but it would be more than her job was worth. Her thoughts flashed to her lunch with Crispin Urquart. She had liked him more as she had got to know him, but his warnings had lingered in her mind.

Something caught her ear. She listened as a caller compared the Prime Minister to Chamberlain. Munich was to Chamberlain what Chequers was to the PM, the caller asserted. Not surprisingly it was not the first time such comparisons had been made. Churchill had described the Munich Agreement in disparaging terms she recalled. The comparison bore scrutiny.

She left her flat and took the tube from Kensington High Street to Sloane Square. As she reached the pavement she looked up at the hoardings. The Royal Court Theatre was showing a play she had wanted to see. She would suggest it to Stella she thought as she walked the short distance to her flat at Cadogan Place.

Stella greeted her. "It's good to see you Maggie. I'm so glad you could make it. You are not the first. I'm expecting a couple more."

She led her inside and placed a drink in her hand. It was a nice flat affording a view over Cadogan Gardens. She remembered how she and Stella had met there, glued to watching 'The Night Manager' a year or two before. Save for a new picture here and there it was much as she remembered it.

"Maggie can I introduce you? This is Oscar and this is Sarah and I think you may know Sally. She is a civil servant also based at Whitehall." The two women looked each other up and down. Maggie did not recognise her.

"I don't think so. There are a lot of us you know," she joked.

"Which department are you?" Sally enquired.

"I was under the Department of Brexit, but now I am seconded to Downing Street," Maggie answered.

Oscar looked at her interestedly. She had not observed him closely up to now. He was six foot or so and nice looking she thought with his dark hair swept back and warm twinkling eyes. He wore a blue shirt open at the collar, jeans and matching blue suede shoes.

It was Sally who spoke. "That must be a little tense right now."

"You could say that," Maggie replied, remaining at least partly non committal.

"Don't get her going on Brexit," interrupted Stella. She recalled their discussion in the Dordogne; their deep conversation at Monpazier about the concessions being made to sell the Chequers offer. She remembered her concerns about Downing Street disregarding the people's will. Their conversation had been confidential, a secret between friends and not to be repeated. She attempted to move the conversation on.

"Did anyone go to the Proms?" she asked as they sat at the dinner table.

"I was there for Beethoven, his fifth I think," Oscar replied.

"One of my favourites," commented Maggie. "That and the seventh. Beethoven reckoned his seventh was perhaps his best I read."

By now the wine was flowing freely. Tongues were loosening and new friendships perhaps being forged. Funny Maggie thought how first impressions counted for so much. She observed the various faces, each making their impression to one another, each taking in each other's signals and responding to them accordingly. Oscar had sat opposite her. Their eyes had met as their conversation had turned to music. It was a subject upon which, like history Maggie could hold her own with just about anyone.

"But tell me more about your work Maggie, it must be very interesting right now?" Oscar spoke nicely, with a hint of a West Country accent.

"I really cannot say much, you will understand I am sure. So much of what we do is confidential related to what is happening in the negotiations," she replied.

"No doubt. Do you feel they are going to plan?" he pressed her.

Maggie thought for a moment before replying.

"To plan?" she repeated. A sneer crossed her face which Oscar noticed. "You could say that, in a sense," she added. She realised she was in danger of opening a Pandora's box and declined to say more.

"But what do you do Oscar?" she asked him, changing the subject. She sipped her wine as their eyes again met across the table.

"Oh, I'm a journalist," he replied. "I write a political column for one of the tabloids. At the moment I'm writing an article upon the moral dilemma of the EU's tariff wall."

Maggie looked at him intrigued. "The moral dilemma?" she asked.

"The moral dilemma of charging our people higher prices for food and clothing bought from poorer countries outside the EU. Countries whose prosperity is being held down by the EU tariff wall making their exports to us more expensive."

With her strong social conscience Maggie had shared the same concerns but instantly the words of Urquart came flooding back. Who knew what comments he might note and duly report if she gave vent to her thoughts?

"That must be interesting, and what about you?" she asked turning to one of the other guests. The conversation swiftly moved on to safer grounds.

The supper did not end late. As she sat in the tube for the short distance back to Kensington High Street her mind ran over the evening. She had enjoyed it. Stella had been an entertaining host laying on a tasty meal and good company. Oscar was an attractive man. In normal circumstances and if she were not seeing Onslow, she would like to see him again. If his occupation had been different then perhaps through Stella she could have engineered the opportunity. But these were not normal times.

As she lay in bed her mind wandered. She wondered how Onslow's evening in Brussels had gone. She thought again of her misgivings: the agreement to concede ever more; to push Chequers no matter how great the deceit; the request Onslow would pursue for the EU to disguise their concessions. She wondered how successful he had been. She thought too of the radio caller comparing Munich to Chequers.

And it was then she remembered that Stella had studied modern history. It was not yet too late. Stella would still be up. She picked up the phone and called her.

"Stella, I hope I'm not ringing too late but thank you for a lovely evening," she said.

"Sure, I'm so glad you could make it Maggie."

Stella listened to her friend as she continued: "Could I ask you something following our conversation in France about the comparisons between Chamberlain and what is happening now? I remember when you were at Cambridge you studied modern British history?"

"Of course. What do you need to know?"

"I heard a caller on the radio comparing the sell out at Chequers to the sell out at Munich. When we were together at Monpazier you quoted Churchill. What did Churchill have to say about Munich? Didn't he castigate it?"

"He did I am sure, but let me call you back tomorrow Maggie. I will check my old notes which I still have. They are filed carefully, don't worry, I am sure I can help you."

Maggie hung up convinced that there were lessons to be learnt not just from her hero Alfred but from Churchill as well. As they had agreed in France there were actually numerous comparisons between the political shenanigans of the late thirties and those of today.

The following day Stella was as good as her word. She had she explained uncovered several things that would be helpful to her friend. When she offered to come round to her flat to go through it Maggie was intrigued. She poured herself a scotch as she waited and threw in some ice. She stood as she so often did when Onslow was due and hovered at the window every now and again glancing along the street. Sure enough she spotted her friend walking briskly, a folder in her arms. Minutes later they sat together as Stella recounted her findings.

"Let me show you Maggie, I think you will rather like this," she announced. There was a trace of excitement in her voice. She opened her notes, many in her own hand taken from her days at Cambridge. She spread them out over the coffee table.

"I have taken the points that I thought may be helpful to you, specifically the correlations between Churchill's reaction to Chamberlain's infamous defence of Munich and what you told me is happening today. He made a great speech on the 5th October 1938 in the House of Commons in which he castigated Munich which he saw as the latest example of the Government's appeasement policy. But look here, Maggie," She pointed to lines from the speech that she had highlighted.

"Churchill actually talks of Alfred and his sons' achievements being then undermined by their successors. He refers to the period of Danegeld and of foreign pressure."

"Sounds familiar!" Maggie interjected.

"But it doesn't stop there. You told me at our dinner at Monpazier about the concessions being made to Brussels. Look what Churchill says here!" She pointed again to the highlighted words and read them aloud.

"The difference between Berchtesgaden, Godesberg and Munich can be simply put. £1 was demanded at the pistol's point. When it was given, £2 was demanded at the pistol's point. Finally the dictator consented to take £1 17s 6d and the rest in promises of goodwill for the future."

Instantly, Maggie stood up unable to contain herself. "That is exactly what is happening now. History is repeating itself," she cried. "They demand one concession after another. We break every law of negotiation by donating rather than exchanging concessions and every time we hit a new bottom line we simply lower it again. We have learned nothing from history!"

She paced the room her mind racing. How much she would like to share this with Crispin she thought.

"There is more," Stella continued. "Look at this." She turned over the sheet upon which she had underlined more sections from the speech.

"He quotes from the Anglo-Saxon Chroniclers allowing their weakness to persist and then 'tells us to take our stand for freedom as in the olden time', again lessons from the past being ignored today."

Stella drank from her glass clearly pleased at Maggie's reaction. Never in all her days at Cambridge had she considered her studies would become relevant in these circumstances, but it had happened and she was beginning to enjoy her friend taking her into her confidence.

Maggie sat down and looked at her. "Did Churchill say anything about the Government being dishonest with the people?"

"Funnily enough he did," she replied. At this Maggie's ears again pricked up. She watched as Stella's pen ran across the notes.

"Here it is. This is where Churchill criticised the Prime Minister and the Government for having failed to re arm despite the growing threats." Again Maggie's eye followed the great man's words. Stella continued her explanation.

"He excoriated them for having kept the truth from the British people which by this time was beginning to leak out. 'They should know that we have sustained a defeat without a war, the consequences of which will travel far with us along our road.' And as we know, his words were prophetic. He uses the term 'pretend' twice, accusing the Government of pretending to the people that all was well in respect of parity of arms with Germany, in other words deceiving them Maggie. 'Thou art weighed in the balance and found wanting' Churchill tells them. He quoted from Daniel 5, verse 27. It was a stinging attack on Chamberlain."

For a moment the two women were silent, Maggie gob-smacked at Stella's words. Churchill's speech was devastatingly relevant now she realised. The people were being sold a spurious, disingenuous assurance that Chequers offered them what they had voted for, despite Queen's Counsellors and others exposing the truth. But why she asked herself, why this deceit? Because, she knew, Downing Street had believed the Treasury that the economy required such a course of deceptive action, ignoring those economists who advocated taking advantage of the global opportunities the referendum result now offered. In short, their beliefs had legitimised their dishonesty.

She knew enough about the theory of motivation and the art of negotiating to write a treatise on the subject. She knew that the avoidance of what could happen was a stronger motivator to the defeatists than the positives that could be accrued by taking the alternative route with its endless and abundant opportunities. The defeatists were winning, drowned in their pool of doubt while those whose minds were set with higher aspirations were being denied.

She thought of Alfred's great defiance speech. She thought of his vision and hope, the promises in his case sincerely meant. When Stella had left she sat back taking comfort from her hero. What a duo Churchill and Alfred would have made she thought, 1100 years apart but both intent upon the most noble of aims, that of securing their people's freedom. She had seen on YouTube the great debaters in the seventies on Brexit. She had marvelled at their perceptive arguments, no more so than Powell. But where were the great speeches of today, she asked herself, where were the politicians willing and able to apply their minds with the sagacious perceptive of a Churchill or a Powell?

She opened her book and read more of her hero Alfred.

May 878

That Whitsun weekend of 878, Alfred found himself at the head of more than 3,500 men. Of these the vast majority were not his professional warriors bearing at least some semblance of weaponry. Certainly those with armour were few to be seen, the vast majority of those rising to the call being the farmers, the peasants and the good folk that had rallied to his call.

By contrast the Great Heathen Army of Guthrum was composed of his professional soldiers; hardened fighting men armed and well practiced in the art of killing. Some were mounted giving them the ability to move quickly and gain the element of surprise. Word had now reached Guthrum that Alfred, the man who had defied him for so long, was on the move.

The destruction of Ubba's Viking army in Devon had been a major setback to him. They had been the forces he had relied upon to make up for his losses a year previously. The strategy of a pincer movement from both the north and the west, trapping and destroying Alfred's forces had evaporated. As Guthrum pondered upon his tactics he recalled just how costly those losses had been. His mind went back to Wareham when he and Alfred had faced one another. He recalled how his fleet of some 120 longships had used

Brownsea Island as their base from where they could see the Anglo-Saxon forces at Poole and Sandbanks cowering, not daring to take them on. But he recalled too how as he had moved on to Exeter expecting to meet the fleet there, but how they had perished off Swanage in that terrible storm of 877. The loss of several thousand men could have been made up had Ubba won the day in Devon. But their destiny had been otherwise.

Yet as Guthrum's spies alerted him to Alfred's advance from Somerset he retained his confidence. This impudent fellow, this king of Wessex who unlike the kings of Mercia, East Anglia and Northumbria had refused to yield would now pay the price. Already he had gained the support of Alfred's fifth column, those aldermen and collaborators who had succumbed to his entreaties; those defeatists who were happy in their own self interest to accept the Viking stranglehold and turn a blind eye to their loss of freedom. Alfred too knew of these men happy to allow the Vikings to remain; happy perhaps to refer to them with a soubriquet that befitted them.

However, Guthrum was well aware that there were still many who had been inspired by Alfred. His spies had confirmed that many of the west Saxon men had said no to promises offered by the Vikings of an accommodation; an accommodation based upon the Viking self interest, the payment of monies to them and compliance to the Viking ways enforceable by the threat of slaughter. This compliance made habitual over 40 years or more had proved a reliable income stream to fund the Viking cause and whenever their purses had run low, the Vikings had come back and demanded more.

Yet if Alfred could be beaten then the whole of Wessex would fall to him from Cornwall to Thanet and up to the Thames bordering the kingdom of Mercia already under Viking control. But if the epic battle to come went in Alfred's favour and the Viking aim of dominance be broken, then such aspirations of freedom might be re awakened in the other kingdoms too. That was a risk he could not afford.

Guthrum knew as Alfred did that upon this battle the very future of England rested and the lot of future generations lay in the hand of destiny. He had not underestimated Alfred however. He recognised his cunning and his audacity as a brave and strategic commander. He had seen how Alfred had managed his sparse resources against the Viking armies. The painful defeat by Alfred and his brother Ethelred at Ashdown after Alfred had marshalled his forces at Windsor had left a stain still to be forgotten that now needed to be expunged. That victory of Alfred had been seven long years ago and still the scars ran deep; still the painful humiliation lay seared within their souls.

Once therefore his spies had confirmed Alfred's advance, Guthrum moved immediately departing his base at Chippenham; that base he had occupied since Alfred's hasty departure on that 12th night after Christmas not five months ago. Leaving only a small contingent behind he rapidly led his forces south strengthening his numbers by bringing in his raiding parties from across Wessex. He would intercept Alfred's army without delay.

Meanwhile Alfred had not tarried long at Egbert's Stone near the little village of Kingston Deverill. He dared not wait in the hope of stragglers joining them. Guthrum's spies would know of his movements. He needed to move quickly and gain the initiative. After just one night as dawn came up, he led his men a few miles north where they settled near the village of Sutton Veney at a place called Iley Oak. It was a well known meeting point; indeed the meeting point for two of the 'hundreds', the administrative units within the regions. To the north the meandering River Wylye offered protection against any surprise attack Alfred realised, though he was as yet uncertain precisely of Guthrum's whereabouts. That evening he waited for his scouts to reappear determined to maintain his army's new found inspiration and momentum.

However, just a few miles away Guthrum was now receiving alarming reports of Alfred's advance. Rumours and sightings of men moving along ancient trackways gathering to Alfred's cause had been rife over the previous weeks and now the latest reports again confirmed: Alfred was on the move.

Now Guthrum led his Great Heathen Army on, like his nemesis Alfred moving forward with an urgency commensurate with the epic battle that was to come. Ahead of them lay the great Iron Age hill fort known as Bratton Camp near the village of Edington. At its centre lay the immense Neolithic long-barrow which for centuries before Alfred's time had been the burial ground for the Saxons too. Alfred could recall his father had been to this place. Edington had become a royal estate. It had a significance for him and for his Saxon followers that would make any victory all the sweeter.

The ancient camp standing on the north western rim of the great Salisbury Plain stood resplendent, its manmade earthen ramparts looking down hundreds of feet upon the surrounding farmland. It was from this commanding strategic position that the Viking army took up its position enabling them to gaze down from the heights upon Alfred's approaching forces. In arriving first Guthrum had given himself the advantage, commanding the high ground and making it all but impossible for Alfred if he chose, to outflank him.

Refusing to be downcast Alfred perceived his cunning plan.

Chapter 11

Autumn 2018

Maggie walked briskly to her office, a number of tasks for the day competing in her mind for prominence. Amongst them was her wish to see Onslow after his return from Brussels. She had called him earlier but he had not picked up nor returned her call. She resolved to try later but in the meantime she was intent upon catching up with Crispin Urquart. Lingering in her mind were the revelations about Churchill she had discussed with Stella and her wish at the very least to make them known to him.

And it was Urquart's voice she recognised as she passed by an open door. Raised voices could be heard within and clearly a serious argument had broken out. She paused intrigued and listened, discreetly out of sight. It was definitely Urquart's voice she was sure and the other voice she knew was that of Sir Stephen Dawkins. For several seconds she tried to fathom what was being said. But it was not her business she told herself and quickly walked on.

Ensconced in her office she turned over her latest files requiring her attention and reeled off half a dozen emails. Why was it she thought that she continued to be plagued by emails copied to her that bore no interest or relevance to her work whatever? The drain upon productivity of such emails across the nation must be something she could not begin to imagine, she conjectured. Nevertheless she answered those she needed with suitable brevity.

A secretary brought in tea and it was as she left the phone rang.

"Maggie, it's Onslow. I think you were trying to reach me. I'm sorry, I've had quite a hectic few days." He sounded cheery, slightly apologetic even, though how sincerely it was meant she could not fathom.

"How are you Onslow, you got back from Brussels a couple days ago didn't you?" she asked him.

There was a pause. "Well last night actually. I decided to stay on an extra night. You know what it's like?"

She made no comment at first. "I wonder if you would like a drink tonight? Let's meet at the usual pub not far from you at Notting Hill say about eight if you like?"

"Fine. Is there anything wrong Maggie?" he ventured.

"Nothing at all. I'll see you then," she answered. She hung up and stared towards the window. Something was wrong she knew but she could not discern what was troubling her. A woman's intuition no doubt but something wrong all the same. Perhaps, she sensed, his time in Brussels had not yielded the results he had hoped for.

She drank the tea and walked toward the window. Outside two pigeons were standing together on a window ledge. She watched for a moment wondering what they too were thinking about. A police car distracted her attention as it suddenly appeared below with its siren wailing. Somehow the traffic parted like the Red Sea opening for the escaping Israelites and the car raced on. London seemed particularly vibrant that day but then to her that was part of the attraction of the great city.

There was a knock on the door. The head of Crispin Urquart appeared.

"Maggie could I have a word with you?" Instantly she detected the anxiety in his voice. He sounded flustered, presumably from the row she had overheard.

"Come in," she said at once. "I was going to speak to you. What is it Crispin?"

He stepped in and walked straight to the open window. As he spoke he kept his back to her. "I've just had a blazing row with Dawkins," he said. Clearly Urquart was struggling to contain his emotions.

Maggie pretended not to have known and said nothing.

"The thing is Maggie, Chequers is not going anywhere. It is disliked by Brussels and is despised by many in the Conservative Party. The trouble is the PM has expended a great deal of capital and either cannot or will not change course. I fear the latter. As everybody knows, Chequers is essentially a travesty of Downing Street's promises of taking back control of our laws, our borders and our money. The answer is to resurrect the Canada style free trade deal Downing Street abandoned, or to go with World Trade Organisation rules as we do with America and China and numerous other countries. But Sir Stephen is so beholden to Downing Street he cannot bring himself to even recommend it."

Urquart was acutely aware of the fact that since the nineties Britain's exports to countries under WTO terms had risen three times as fast as trade with the single market, a fact ignored or unknown by the pro European establishment. As a counter to such arguments terms such as 'cliff edge' and 'crashing out' had been eagerly taken up by the Remainer elements of the media as part of the on-going Project Fear.

At the back of Urquart's mind too were the free trade opportunities that he knew existed but were at present unable to be exploited. In the days of the Empire, Britain had been at the epicentre of the biggest free trade area the world had ever known, comprising one quarter of the globe. Now in the belief Britain would indeed extricate itself from the shackles of Europe, many Commonwealth countries were queuing up to secure new partnerships today. When Britain had eschewed the Commonwealth in favour of the European dream, a prominent Labour Europhile had uttered the words 'we don't do kith and kin politics'. The remark had stuck in the throat of his distinguished Australian listener mindful of how the countries had fought side by side together in defence of the mother country. Today even a small percentage of the Commonwealth countries could form an economic block larger than the EU. Yet such opportunity was being denied whilst Britain remained tied to the European rule book. It was the Remainers happy to maintain such constraints who were the real little Englanders Urquart believed.

He turned and looked at her as if seeking reassurance.

"It's all about leverage," she retorted. "We are not exerting any. Merely being reactive and conciliatory," she said. She too was aware that some Remainer Members of Parliament together with their friends in the Europhile media had taken to describing a 'no deal' – or World Trade Organisation deal – as 'crashing out'. Phrases such as 'cliff edge' had become common place. These pejorative terms had served only to undermine the Prime Minister's leverage. In effect, the

Remainers had sent the PM in to bat for England – but had given her a bat of straw. Brussels had been emboldened as a result. Managing expectations, so crucial to a successful negotiation, had been hugely undermined.

Crispin Urquart had read her thoughts.

"Precisely Maggie! Downing Street has no stomach for leverage. If a Canada style agreement was not forthcoming the PM could say we would introduce the most competitive tax rates in the EU, we would agree trade arrangements with Asia and the US and we would review our regulatory burden. Even according to the EU, if we dropped just seven of the major EU regulations, British companies would save around £6 billion a year. All our companies suffer but less than 10% sell into the EU anyway. It's madness.

He paused waiting for her reaction. Maggie sat back in her chair. A thoughtful expression crossed her face.

"Real leverage as you know Crispin arises from our imports. The billions we spend on French and Italian produce and our enormous imports of German cars and machinery; more exported here than to China and the USA combined. Imagine if we threatened a 10% tariff on all of that. My calculation was that we would take in £10 billion a year: that on top of the billions we will save in payments to Brussels each year. A tariff such as that plus the threat to withhold the £39 billion or more, gives us ample leverage. We have plenty of leverage but we are too afraid to use it."

Crispin nodded vigorously. "There is something else you should know. The Tory Party Conference has not been easy for Downing Street. The party is livid. A tsunami is approaching, the people simply will not wear it. I said to you a Member of Parliament exposing what is going on is the right way to let the cat out of the bag but…" He paused mid sentence.

"But what Crispin, tell me?"

"But when a politician makes such points it is easily derided as simply playing politics. A civil servant on the other hand speaking from the inside carries weight."

At once she interrupted him. "But you told me that this must be avoided; how our jobs might be taken from us and threats under the Official Secrets Act used against us! What are you now saying?"

"I am saying that there may now be no alternative, that you and I may have to go to the press after all. Those who stand up Maggie make a sacrifice and we may be called upon to do that sooner than we think. There may be no alternative. At some stage Downing Street must be held to account."

Maggie thought of Churchill's quote and repeated it aloud. "Thou art weighed in the balance and found wanting."

Crispin looked directly at her. "Sounds like Churchill?" he said.

"Churchill indeed."

"How very apposite!" he remarked. He reached for his black fountain pen she had seen before and wrote down the quote.

"That just might come in useful. The chickens will surely come home to roost." There was something enigmatic in his statement. For the first time Maggie saw the hint of a smile.

* * *

Maggie was back at her flat in Kensington Church Street in good time. In a couple of hours she was due to see Onslow.

She had not seen him for the best part of a week and whilst she realised the tension between them over their approach to the negotiations was real she still had no wish to let it insidiously drive them apart. Despite his shortcomings, Onslow's rakish charm she still found attractive. Yet for some reason she was in no mood to dress up for him. After she had showered she threw on old clothes: he could take her as he found her this evening.

She turned on the television just as the news came on. As always she listened for the headlines. At first nothing especially took her attention but then she turned and looked at the screen.

"Downing Street today reported that the EU were not treating Britain with respect by simply saying no and offering no counter proposals to the Chequers offer," came the announcement.

Maggie sighed as she watched. Just as she had predicted the two sides were digging in. This was all part of the propaganda being fed to the British people, an orchestrated campaign to maintain the illusion that the referendum result was safe in Downing Street's hands; the grand design, the magnificent tapestry of opportunity that lay before the people would not be abandoned. The Government were playing it tough. But she knew it was anything but and she cringed at what she was hearing.

She turned away and opened the fridge and pulled from it a dish she could microwave quickly. She was not especially hungry and anyway time was short. As she ate she checked her latest emails. Nothing important required her attention thank goodness, only a brief note from Stella to say she would call her tonight. She wondered what it was about but gave it no further thought as she began the walk up Kensington Church Street a few minutes later. The pub was not far and almost exactly half way to Onslow's place in Notting Hill.

She stared at the buildings taking in their individual design as she walked. Her grandfather had lived in one before the war though she knew not which. Her previous flat at Argyll Road close by had been pleasant enough. Her mind swirled back to those happy days as she felt the breeze in her face. She had shared the place with Amanda and Sam, two of her oldest friends. It was time she called them she thought.

When she reached the pub she ventured in but Onslow was nowhere to be seen. She walked out to the attractive courtyard garden full of people chatting merrily on the terraces. On a late summer's evening in London this was surely one of her favourite haunts.

"Maggie," a voice called. She turned around. It was not Onslow but instantly she recognised the face of a female friend she had not seen for a while. They exchanged pleasantries as her eye kept searching for her quarry. Angie was about her age and blest with attractive looks. They had played squash together in the past and it was good to catch up. Nevertheless they had not remained close. For some reason Maggie had always held her at arm's length.

When Onslow entered, she spotted him immediately. He was still in a suit. He embraced her and kissed her on the cheek. Maggie looked at him taking in his demeanour. He seemed less relaxed than usual. She watched as he ran his hands through his hair waiting to be introduced to her friend.

"It's nice to meet you," he said charmingly, shaking Angie's hand. His arm was around Maggie's waist but the eye contact between the two of them was immediately picked up by the ever observant Maggie.

"So how are you Onslow? I haven't seen you for a little while," she asked him.

She detected a sheepish look from him as if reticent to say too much.

"I'm fine. It has been a busy time that's all."

"What do you do?" enquired Angie. Maggie noted her looking him up and down.

"Oh I am in the Civil Service like Maggie. We work together in Whitehall."

"And sometimes out of Whitehall," Maggie interjected. She was eager to know of his time in Brussels. He grinned but said nothing.

"Well, it's been nice meeting you Onslow. I have to go. Perhaps we'll meet again." Angie made her excuses and left them alone.

Over the next hour they talked over several drinks. Strangely, Maggie thought, Onslow was not overly forthcoming about his Brussels trip. When she asked him directly about the EU's willingness to cover up the British concessions he revealed only that they would consider it. His words unbeknown to her were true enough. She pushed him no more but the subject of leverage that had dominated her discussions with Crispin still played upon her mind. At length she broached the subject.

"There never was any intention of exerting leverage," he told her.

He saw the look of exasperation come over her face. Onslow continued as if to ram home the point.

"Do you remember when Cameron made his Bloomberg speech announcing that he would go to Brussels and negotiate a better deal and then advocate we stay in the EU at the referendum?" he asked her.

"I remember it well," Maggie replied.

"Well, the political commentator asked him if then he would advocate against staying in the EU if he did not win a better deal. Cameron declined to say he would. There never has been a wish to exert leverage Maggie, and all of us have gone along with it; all of us that is except you and Crispin Urquart."

Maggie looked aghast. "So negotiating a deal for Britain that was true to Brexit in line with the people's wishes has never been on the agenda Onslow?" she retorted.

"Of course not, it's not about what the people want, it's what the establishment wants. It's what Downing Street wants. It's what the Treasury wants. It's what the CBI wants and that's all there is to it. We just have to play the game."

Later that evening Maggie sat disconsolately playing Onslow's words over again and again in her mind. She need not have been shocked at his revelation. It had only been confirmation of what she already knew. But now she had heard it: heard it from someone with whom she had an intimate relationship and was close to the top. Lost in thought she opened her book unable to put off reading of Alfred's impending battle any longer. Her own battles were as nothing, of course. Yet Onslow's words played upon her mind. She barely heard the phone ring. Eventually she picked it up and listened.

"Maggie, is that you? It's Stella."

Jarred out of her thoughts she recalled the message Stella

had left earlier. It was nice to hear her voice. There was a hint of excitement in her tone.

"Listen, I have done some further reading up. I have a bit more insight on Churchill and Munich." For a minute or two she added flesh to their earlier conversation. Maggie listened with interest.

"Oh by the way, you certainly made a hit the other night at the supper," she added.

"What do you mean, Stella?"

"With Oscar, he's asked me for your phone number. I hope you don't mind Maggie but I gave it to him. He's such a nice guy."

Chapter 12

May 878

The darkness had descended that evening at Iley Oak. It would be their only night there Alfred had told them and when that night turned to day the future for all Wessex would be determined. Ellie looked across the rows of camp fires stretched in all directions around them. She wondered what the men sat beside each would be thinking. Perhaps they shared her mixed emotions: exuberant joy at having come together under Alfred's banner buoyed up and inspired by his stirring words but in the knowledge too that for many this would be their final night on this earth.

Alfred had issued his orders and conjured up the tactics to be deployed. Their advance would be along the narrow ridge towards the highest point taking the gradient at its most shallow assent. The front lines would lock shields as a wall intent upon driving all before them. Behind them one line back, spears would be thrown over their heads; javelins landing upon the Vikings forcing them to give way. Like two wrestlers locked together the victory would go to the side which forced the issue finding the weakest point. They would move as one, not dissipating their strength but confident in the knowledge that if each man united with his brothers heaving their massed weight together as one, the day would be theirs.

"I need to talk to as many as I can this night," Alfred said to Ellie. "I need to be amongst them." She understood and watched as he left her to walk amongst the little camp fires.

As the evening wore on, men sitting together in clusters looked up recognising him and at each he sat and shared their thoughts, listening to their concerns, their hopes, their dreams and passing words of confidence that all would be well. Inside he shared their fears but never once did Alfred show it. Their confidence, their belief and their sheer determination to see the issue through was what mattered. To those whose fear seemed to overcome them he held them close to him so they felt his presence personally and took comfort from it. If glory could be defined as overcoming odds through bravery and resolve in support of the most noble cause, then the glory would surely be theirs.

Slowly Alfred went from little fire to little fire, through small bands of armed men, some sharpening their spears, some praying, others able to sleep finding respite before the morn. Fathers and sons sat together, the former intent upon giving confidence to their sons; a confidence despite for many having experienced the slaughter of previous battles. Alfred's presence amongst them, his behaviour confirming their unity and hope in this great unfolding drama, left its mark – this little touch of Alfred in the night.

When later he tried to sleep, a silent prayer entered his head as Ellie lay beside him. He prayed not only for victory but that he himself would remain fit and strong for the great ordeal. Tomorrow he would need all his strength he knew.

As dawn rose during that second week of May it was Ellie

who woke first. It had been a long night. She had tried to sleep but somehow it had evaded her as her furtive mind had imagined the battle to come. She leant across her sleeping Alfred and stared at his face. How handsome his features were she thought, not grimaced or made older by the stresses he had endured but still reflecting the radiance of his youth. She let her hand slide down over his chest feeling his gentle intake of breath as he sensed her presence in his sleep. Nothing must happen to his body she thought: somehow her beloved Alfred must come through this great ordeal unscathed even if the victory were to elude him.

He had insisted she stay well back from the fray but she knew the terrible sights and sounds would be almost too much to bear. Only if and when the battle was won did she know it would be safe to go forward. Several times in the past Ellie had done so. She had witnessed the awful sight of bewildered womenfolk stepping through the dead and dying, intrepidly seeking out their loved ones. She had seen the corpses lying sometimes two or three deep their limbs missing, their blood still spilling over the grass turning it into a scarlet tapestry of hell on earth. She had seen the women crying uncontrollably as their worst fears had been confirmed. She had seen too those men and women scouring the battlefields, scavengers rifling through the clothes for anything of value; their wounded targets impotent, unable to resist, crying out in their death throes.

Alfred had encouraged her to pray. She had become accustomed to his passion for his Christian faith inveighed upon him and nourished since as a boy he had visited Rome. It was a faith she shared. To choose to believe; to choose to pray; to choose to accept they were not alone but were overseen by a loving God no matter their travails was what he had taught her. She moved her hand to his forehead and let it rest lightly without waking him as she prayed silently for his safety. Not only safety but victory; victory at all costs, victory despite all they had been through, victory as reward for all his defiance, victory to secure the freedom of all his people. As she finished her prayer he opened his eyes and looked lovingly at her. His hand found hers. A smile of reassurance emitted from his lips as he read her thoughts.

She returned the smile and kissed him delicately on the lips. No words needed to be spoken: indeed to have spoken at that moment would have been to break the spell; to have driven a knife through a painting of the most sublime beauty. The silence between them somehow stood out as a beacon of defiance, a stark and audacious contrast to the noise and commotion that would shortly erupt. Only after they had each allowed their kiss to linger did she whisper to him her words of love.

He clutched her closer to him as if again reassuring her that his strength would prevail.

"Have faith my love," he said quietly. He knew the lines from the book of Joshua and now they came tumbling from his lips: "Do not be afraid Ellie, the Lord is with us."

She took comfort from the words. These were not simply vain words of bravado she knew. From Alfred whose faith had remained so solid for so long these were words he genuinely believed, an affirmation of beliefs that he took comfort from and passed to others around him.

She watched as he dressed and strangely those feelings of confidence began to wash over her. Slowly, just slowly she shook off the tensions of the night.

Alfred had insisted they ate. Their strength might depend upon it. Outside he surveyed the scene. He looked across his gallant army; his band of brothers brought together by destiny for one of history's greatest moments, each man stealing himself for the drama to come.

His mind went back to their Christmas at Chippenham, to the scene of happy faces as they had seen the New Year in and defied Guthrum that winter. He thought of their sudden escape that night, the twelfth night when Guthrum had without warning gained the initiative advancing from his base at Gloucester. He remembered their plight, the months they had endured making their way to the safety of Athelney. He had had his expectations challenged alright, he told himself. He had faced the powers of hell, the very gates of Hades. But he had faced them down and today would be their reward; the day he would turn his vision of freedom into a reality, the day his people would throw off the Viking yoke. His blood was up, his confidence high. After all, he Alfred had defeated the Vikings at Ashdown. He had done it before. He could do it again and today his dreams of freedom would be made manifest.

A little later high up on the narrow ridge that formed the summit to Bratton Camp, Guthrum looked down watching as Alfred now began to move his men around towards the gentler gradient. He was confident. He knew the majority of those who had rallied to Alfred's cause were artisans, farmers and the like armed not with swords, but staves and pitchforks and the occasional axe. By comparison his own men were hardened fighters used to the parry and thrust of battle, the need to get their own blow in first. Moreover his men benefitted from rounded helmets and a modicum of armour offering a protection most of Alfred's men could only dream of. The battle to come would be his he was sure. After all, the Viking onslaught for the last ninety years had with few exceptions been overwhelming. Mercia, Northumbria and East Anglia had all succumbed and today this thorn in the side, this audacious commander who dared still to defy him would be brought to heel.

Below him on the lower slopes Alfred was now moving closer. The end of the long ridge was within sight and soon their ascent would begin. Alfred studied the ground judging the moment to begin their turn. He knew there was no chance to outflank the Viking army occupying as it did the entire width of the narrow ridge. The battle would be contested with the two forces directly facing each other, as the lines drew closer each man seeing their own personal adversaries coming into view. If any man in Alfred's brave force now felt his courage leaving him, withdrawal was not an option as the lines tightened, their shields drawn together, an interlocking wall of men moving inexorably forward to triumph or disaster.

Alfred looked up, his attention caught by sounds carried upon the breeze. Now the sounds grew a little louder; curses and the steady beating of Viking shields, girding the spirits of their owners for what was to come. This fearsome noise of steel against steel rising above the curses of men; this cacophony of discordant din; this symphony from hell setting his pulse suddenly racing: he knew the psychological effect it could have, the fear that could rend men in two, torn between their allegiance to their king, their honour and pride and the temptation to succumb to terror, defeat or flight.

Alfred had positioned himself at the front in the very centre of his advancing troops: nearly four thousand or so men moving as one, their front ranks now tightly closed allowing no gap between them. Around him rode his most loyal fighting men each willing to lay down their lives to protect their king. If either leader could be destroyed a rout could easily follow. But Alfred could be seen, his banner aloft, rousing his men on above the din like a great conductor leading his orchestra towards its great finale.

Now their lines were drawing closer to the wall of Viking shields, fifty yards still to go. The gentle gradient Alfred had chosen was so far bearable. Their pace remained slow but steady, each man determined to keep their rhythm and not to let their fellows down. Their wall must not be breached Alfred had exhorted them; the lines had to remain locked with their spears interspersed between the wall of shields pointed directly at their targets.

The sounds of drumming on the Viking shields grew louder now, competing with the curses and shouting of men driven on by a toxic mixture of raw adrenaline and animal instincts for survival. Their roaring voices helped to nullify their fear and to instil terror into the hearts of Alfred's troops. But they too responded in like fashion: two teams wrestling now for supremacy, each knowing that upon this epic battle the whole future of Wessex depended. Now the Anglo-Saxons were beating their shields also; a symphony of tense and thrilling anticipation, a prelude to the drama to come. All that Alfred had stood for, the liberty and sovereignty of his people he had promised them, all now depended upon his leadership and resolve. Future generations would look back and history would be his judge.

Guthrum now rose in his saddle staring directly ahead at the oncoming Anglo-Saxon forces gauging their strength, reading their intentions. He shouted orders to his men to raise their shields guarding their heads from projectiles as he saw the wall drawing closer. Each man was now directly ahead of his opposite number his face now clearly in view, each weighing up their likely nemesis as the seconds ticked by.

Then suddenly with just yards to go, Alfred roared his orders above the din for the second lines to hurl their javelins above the heads of those in front. A thousand years later Wellington would issue the same orders as the artillery barrages from behind the lines wrought destruction upon Napoleon's armies and later generals would do likewise liberating the bloodied fields of the western front from the German menace. As the javelins embedded themselves into the Viking shields their guard was dropped exposing many to the waiting Anglo-Saxon spears.

As the two sides clashed the lines still held. Each man now faced his adversary thrusting and parrying blows to the face and upper body; each screaming their anguish as blows struck home. Alfred remained mounted for as long as possible being seen by his men and while he remained alive their spirits rose in reward. As men fell dying from their wounds their place was taken by others determined to keep the wall from being breached. Now Alfred's men were barely moving forward as hand to hand they fought and traded blows. Shields were being wrenched away by spears hooking and pulling back against their rims and as men lost their shield protection they suddenly became vulnerable, their bodies exposed to thrusting swords and scything axes.

141

Now many on both sides lay slain, their gored limbs and entrails exuding blood flowing in little streams upon the turf. Alfred was turning in all directions shouting and exhorting his men on, his sword raining blows, cutting, scything and thrusting relentlessly. All around men were falling, their terrible cries piercing the still spring air. Far below Ellie looked up at the ridge of death. Her mind was racing, trying desperately to take control but as with a nightmare, unable to influence the outcome, unable to bring it to an end; unable to do anything but succumb to whatever destiny commanded. The waiting felt interminable to her knowing as she did that with every minute scores of men were being horribly mutilated and slain. But all she could do was pray and put her trust in God.

For a long time the battle continued. This was no short lived affair, but a mighty tussle; two armies refusing to give way, the one of armoured fighting men, the other driven only by their resolve, spurred on by their inspiring leader to rid themselves of their tormentors. And it was this sheer dogged determination that was beginning to pay off. As exhaustion set in it was the Vikings whose shield wall broke, opening the gap for Alfred's men suddenly emboldened to renew their ferocity. More men started to pile in as they sensed fresh hope, their spirits high as if mirroring Alfred's banner flying proudly aloft signifying defiance and victory within their grasp. And as they did so the Viking army finally gave way. Many turned and tried to flee only to be chased and cut down mercilessly, their bodies left for human and animal scavengers to go about their sordid business.

Somehow Guthrum and his personal guard, the elite of what had been the Great Heathen Army now being decimated and destroyed, made their escape on horseback. As Alfred saw them flee he knew he had to give chase. Yes the victory, the great and glorious victory he had dreamt of was actually his. His people were on the edge of achieving the freedom that had eluded them for so long, yet if Guthrum were allowed to escape then surely it would only be a matter of time before another great battle would ensue. He had seen Guthrum get away before only to wage war against him later. Now Alfred was determined those lessons from history would be acted upon. This time it would be different. This time the Viking menace would be properly contained and his people's freedom assured. This time there would be no fudge and acceptance that somehow the matter would be settled at a later date. And so it was that Alfred, exhausted but victorious, exultant at having turned his defiance, the ignominy of his hiding in the marshes of Somerset into the most momentous victory, now set off in pursuit.

The victory had been won – but the peace had not yet been secured.

Autumn 2018

Maggie Taylor had put her book down. She stood and gazed out of her flat window at nothing in particular. Alfred's story had inspired her. Politicians had begun to talk of settling for Chequers and then somehow at some distant and unknown point in the future trying again to secure a proper freedom. How different to Alfred's approach she thought. If only they too had shown the determination to see the matter through rather than opt for what one principled opponent of the Prime Minister had termed a constitutional outrage, a moral and intellectual humiliation. Her mind flickered again to Chamberlain and Churchill; to her conversation with Stella; to their comparison of the current situation to that of Munich.

She turned and poured herself a scotch always her reliable fixer calculated to relieve the stresses of the day. She sat and opened her laptop sensing the need to distract her thoughts.

Then as Maggie scoured her emails something of interest caught her eye. It was from Sir Stephen Dawkins headed 'Confidential'. She read it carefully as she always did with anything bearing his name. It was brief but to the point. He was it stated, putting together a report for Downing Street summarising their negotiation position and asking her to make any submissions she cared to. The request was to four other colleagues as well. She glanced down the list of names. All were supportive of the policies proposed and accepted by Downing Street. Onslow Ratcliffe was amongst them she noted. Crispin Urquart's name was noted for its absence.

She leant back in her chair and stared at the window trying to discern Dawkins' motives. She had not argued with Sir Stephen in the same way as Crispin but there was no doubt he saw her attitude as unhelpful. Perhaps his intention was to diffuse her anger, to placate her with the pretence her opinion counted. But perhaps that was too cynical an interpretation: if his request was sincerely intended then this was at the very least an opportunity to convey her misgivings in writing. She determined to expend time on it. He would have her submission without delay.

Later that evening as she showered Maggie heard her mobile ringing. She could easily leave it she thought but something made her throw a towel around her and shuffle to the phone.

"Hello, is that Maggie?" came a man's voice. For a moment she did not answer. But then she recognised the West Country accent.

"Yes, can I help you?" she replied.

"Maggie, this is Oscar. You remember we met at Stella's supper party. I hope you don't mind me calling. How are you?"

She smiled to herself relieved her suspicions were confirmed. He had a nice way of speaking she remembered, charming but polite and sincere at the same time.

"I'm fine thank you. It's nice to speak to you again. What can I do for you Oscar?"

"Well, I was wondering if we could perhaps get together sometime? I'd love to see you again and get to talk to you."

Maggie hesitated immediately reminding herself of Crispin Urquart's words of warning about speaking to members of the press. But he had given her mixed messages. She prevaricated knowing all the while that she would like nothing more than to see him, not only socially but to tell him anything he might like to know. However, the temptation to say too much if they met might be too great.

Politely she declined the offer making an excuse of work overload which was true enough. She detected the note of disappointment in his voice but when he promised to call another time she heard herself consenting. Maggie put the phone down wondering if she had done the right thing but as the evening wore on convinced herself she had. She ruminated about Oscar's motives though, playing over his words in her mind. Perhaps the attraction she had felt towards him was mutual but Crispin's words were haunting her. She had been right to err on the side of caution she told herself.

That same evening the red Porsche of Onslow Ratcliffe was parked outside a chic restaurant in Chelsea. Inside Ratcliffe sat in a discreet corner, a medium rare cooked sirloin steak in front of him and a half empty glass of claret. Sat opposite him was Sir Stephen Dawkins.

"The Northern Ireland backstop issue is going rather well Stephen, don't you think?" Onslow declared. His words were more a statement than a question.

Dawkins sipped his wine and replied with a hint of glee in his voice. "Indeed, the EU is playing it as an obstacle to progress for all they are worth, just as we intended when we made such a generous concession to them last December."

He recalled how Downing Street had conceded the backstop ensuring no hard border and the province, like the republic, effectively remaining within the customs union. The rest of the UK would have to do the same if the union was to be preserved. The Brexiteers had expressed severe doubts: it was merely a form of words they had been disingenuously assured; simply to move the negotiation along. It had proved anything but, providing massive leverage for the EU.

A wry smile emanated from Dawkins' lips as he savoured the satisfaction of his words. "So accommodating of Downing Street to go along with our little ruse!"

"Quite so," replied Onslow. "Just as we hoped the backstop will see off any talk of a Canada style free trade agreement and keep us tied to their coat strings, either that or ensure another referendum."

Dawkins poured the remaining contents of the bottle into their glasses.

"Here's to a deep and special partnership," he toasted as they touched glasses. At that moment Onslow's phone rang.

"Excuse me would you Stephen, I had better take it," he said.

His face lit up as he recognised Ingrid's sexy voice. Their conversation was short and to the point. Francois she told him, wished to meet with him in two days time in Brussels to discuss her request concerning the cover up. Afterwards she invited him to stay over. Onslow maintained his calm demeanour aware Dawkins could hear his every word. He confirmed the arrangement and put the phone away.

"You have good news from Brussels, Onslow if I am not mistaken?"

Both men smiled. "It would seem so," Onslow replied laconically.

"Do whatever you have to do," Dawkins added.

Onslow nodded. "Indeed, for Queen and country of course."

"Of course. To Queen and country," Dawkins retorted. They raised their glasses again, a look of smug satisfaction etched upon their faces.

Chapter 13

Autumn 2018

The Friday evening could not have come soon enough for Maggie. Almost a month had passed since her weekend with Stella in the Dordogne. It seemed to her much longer as she sat in the traffic on the M3 and played the happy memories over in her mind. She needed to get out of London, to find release and above all, a distraction from Brexit that had so consumed her thoughts. Three of her oldest school friends had invited her to spend a couple of days walking a section of the South West coast path in Dorset and she had relished the opportunity. As a girl her parents had taken her regularly to the South Hams and she knew parts of the coast path well but had never walked it in the lovely county of Dorset. The fresh sea air after the recent stifling heat of London would do her good she knew.

It was to her parents' house in Bournemouth that Maggie was now headed having promised to break the journey and spend an evening with them. She knew how lucky she was to have them still in reasonable health. They were a close family. When David and Jill Taylor had moved from London to the coast Maggie had promised she would visit them regularly and she had been as good as her word.

The traffic had started to move again. She nudged her beloved Beetle forward holding off a driver attempting to cut in. She was in no mood to give way to aggression. It was then she noticed the sign to Winchester: immediately she thought of Alfred with its long history and association with her hero. She imagined him walking the old main street and the Vikings there as they had been. She smiled as she thought of Alfred's almost miraculous turnaround from the dark days at Athelney to his immense victory at Edington. Maggie knew it wasn't the end of the story and that evening she would open her book once more.

When later she duly arrived, her father put his arms around her and welcomed her inside. David Taylor was the epitome of a genteel, quintessential Englishman; indeed in Maggie's eyes he could do little wrong, always there for her, always fussing about her welfare, always a role model and man of integrity. To him however, she was a girl alone in the big city.

Nevertheless, he had a profound confidence and affection for his daughter. She had excelled at Cambridge; she was independently minded and as he knew, well capable of standing up to the slings and arrows of outrageous fortune. David Taylor had studied politics: indeed it ran in the family. He often recalled Margaret Thatcher's maxim that only those who never tried to achieve anything escaped without criticism. He had however, little idea how apt those words might prove to his daughter that evening. He had wanted to ask her about her work in Whitehall but had never pushed her to reveal more than she ought. Yet he was conscious too she needed a listener, someone she could confide in, and that was one of the requisites of a good father.

As they walked through to the garden her mother Jill turned and smiled as she spotted her daughter. Together they made tea and sat on the terrace overlooking the freshly cut lawn.

"Darling, Dad and I have a little surprise for you," her mother said.

Maggie looked at her curiously. Her mother had retained her good looks, her features still attractive despite the advancing years. She had continued to dress elegantly, never pretentiously, but always taking care over her appearance.

It was her father who spoke. "The Bournemouth Symphony Orchestra is playing Sibelius tonight at the Pavilion. We know how much you love Sibelius so we thought we'd go. We can leave in good time and get a bite to eat nearby if you like."

The announcement had its desired effect. A smile spread across Maggie's pretty features; a smile of surprise and of genuine pleasure.

Later she took a shower and began to dress for the evening. It was then her phone rang. She looked down at it on the bed for some reason hesitating before picking it up. She recognised the voice instantly.

"Maggie, I hope you will forgive me for calling you again. It's Oscar."

Despite her earlier put off she was pleased to receive his call.

"Of course. It's nice to speak to you Oscar," she said to him.

"Listen Maggie, I know you told me you were pretty tied up right now but I've been given tickets for a play, the new one at the Royal Court at Sloane Square. I know it's a long shot, but I was wondering if you would like to come along."

His voice sounded attractive as it had previously, sincere and warm. She remembered seeing the advertisements as she had ascended the tube at Sloane Square whilst walking to Stella's dinner. It was a coincidence she thought but a happy one. This time she relented.

"Alright, thank you Oscar. That would be great."

As he replied she detected his obvious pleasure at her response.

"It's next Wednesday a little after 7.00. Let's meet there. Thank you Maggie, it will be a great evening."

After the call she sat quietly on her bed. Again the warning of Crispin came back to haunt her. However, the words of Onslow at the pub when he had confessed there never was any intention of respecting the people's will played upon her mind even more. Her anger at what her civil servant and political colleagues were engaged in; the great betrayal as she had termed it, had reached fever pitch. At some point the truth would become known. Already politicians at the Conservative Conference were openly disparaging Downing Street's insistence upon sticking to Chequers. 'Chuck Chequers' had become the cry of thousands. She thought of her conversations with Stella. Chequers was to Downing Street what Munich had been to Chamberlain she knew – a shameful dishonest episode in the nation's history.

The tension now between herself and Onslow was real and like the negotiations themselves perhaps in danger of break down. Whilst she would not speak to Oscar of the negotiations she told herself, she would at least allow herself to simply enjoy this man's company.

That evening Maggie Taylor sat beside her parents in the dress circle of the Bournemouth Pavilion. She watched the orchestra tuning up, listening to the strange noises as one instrument competed with another making oddly contrasting sounds. She looked up at the domed roof. The place could do with a coat of paint she noticed. But soon enough the milestone of a centenary year would arise and no doubt then it would be restored to its former glory.

Soon she was lost in the music, her mind totally absorbed as she took in the great melodies. However, it was in the second half that the climax to the evening was to come. For this was her favourite: Sibelius' second symphony, the one that Classic FM never seemed to play. She loved the music: the glorious melodies and the pulsating climaxes repeatedly asserting themselves like the great waves outside pounding the shore relentlessly. Not once did she think of Onslow; not once of the phone call from Oscar with whatever significance it might hold; not once of the tumultuous negotiations with which she wrestled. At length the final movement came with its emotive finale moving all before it. She sank back in her seat and let that moment when you thought the orchestra had no more to give, but were instead transported to the heavens, overcome her.

Her father glanced at his daughter as she sat transfixed. David Taylor had been an experienced public speaker in his career. For him the symphony could have been Churchill's soaring oratory put to music. The sonorous growling bass tones followed by exquisitely repeated rhythmic phrasing interspersed by great rolling cadences rising to double forte. The injection of pathos that public speakers had perfected since the days of Aristotle seemed in the music to have reached unsurpassed levels. Hardly before the sound had abated the audience was on its feet showing their approval; wild applause echoing down from the great domed roof.

Later that evening Maggie lay in her bed totally relaxed, her brain freed of all its concerns. When she awoke she enjoyed a leisurely breakfast with her parents and set off to join her friends for their walk along the coast path. Over the next two days together they covered over twenty miles chatting merrily and never once discussing Brexit.

Yet it was only a temporary relief. When at last she returned to her flat in London normality quickly asserted itself. Somehow she had resisted opening her emails but now as she sat back on her sofa a scotch in hand, she couldn't resist it any longer. One was from Onslow saying he had to spend another couple of days in Brussels. She sipped from the glass as she contemplated when she might see him again. But she did not dwell on it. Another email caught her eye. It was a gentle reminder from Sir Stephen for her submission to the negotiation report he had requested.

Maggie had not forgotten. It was due the next day and she had already written half of it and had planned to complete it tonight. For the umpteenth time she began to contemplate the key points to include. Brevity needed to be observed and plenty of tact as well.

She had set out a comprehensive strategy to alter their negotiating approach even at this late stage. But in doing so she had also outlined the litany of errors often resulting from directives from Downing Street. She had listed the endless unconditional concessions; the lack of proper vision; the low entry positions; the jettisoning of bottom lines; the mismanagement of expectations; the dreadful preparation; the Treasury's desperation which had so undermined them; the failure to exert any hint of leverage; the agreement to the Irish backstop which had enabled their adversaries to exert such leverage; the swathes of law to be subjected to a common rule book overseen by the ECJ; the resultant inability to accept the recent offer of a trade deal with the USA; the emasculation of global free trade opportunities; the enormous promises of cash in return for nothing; the pretence that this was Brexit when it fact it was Brino; the agreement to sequencing issues which had so undermined their ability to claw back and use their variables cleverly – and so much more. The maxim repeated by Downing Street that nothing is agreed until everything is agreed she knew had been little more than empty rhetoric.

But as she began to write she knew only too well the points she was making, no matter how tactfully put, would not go down well. Her mind turned to Alfred and the lessons she had gleaned: his vision and his defiance; his inspiration and his leadership; his refusal to keep conceding and his resolve to regain his people's freedom. The parallels albeit in different circumstances were nevertheless uncanny; yet the outcomes so very different. The follies in their negotiation had been manifold and in some cases intentional, amounting to a sordid collusion between senior politicians in government and the top echelon of the civil service. But to even hint at such things would hardly be a propitious career move.

Yet in her father's tradition duty and integrity were to Maggie the values she needed to live by and to settle for less somehow would devalue her. Besides she was a patriot. To many today the word seemed somehow old fashioned. But a patriot she was, nurtured by her knowledge of history and the lives that had been laid down in earlier times in her island story in their quest for freedom.

Two hours later she flopped into her bed and tried to free

her mind. There was only one antidote she knew. She sank back on her pillow and read of Alfred.

May 878

All across the high narrow ridge upon which the epic Battle of Edington had taken place gored bodies lay, a scene of the most harrowing destruction. Ellie surveyed the awful picture in her own way mirroring the words that Wellington was to say nearly a thousand years later as he recalled the field of Waterloo, 'Nothing except a battle lost can be half so melancholy as a battle won'. Ellie was not alone. She stood and stared with other women folk tentatively looking on. She saw those who frantically plundered the dead and dying taking their primitive shoes; emptying pockets of torn and bloodied garments; searching for anything of value; pulling rings off fingers from those too wounded to resist. The Vikings had worn their spoils. At least they were returning into Anglo-Saxon hands she told herself.

As the late afternoon breeze swept across Bratton Camp, the place resembled a scene from hell littered with faces some decapitated from their bodies, a look of horror etched for posterity, destined to remain seared in the memories of those who came across them. She saw the torn arms and limbs, blood still issuing from them. She saw the bodies a thousand or was it many more, impaled with arrows and spears where they fell.

The cathartic joy that the victors felt after all the horror and despair they had endured was overwhelming but as they surveyed this awful scene they were reminded of the huge sacrifices they had made: mindful perhaps to the astute Ellie, that the only way to respect that sacrifice was to preserve their new found freedom in the future, never to let it go; never to allow again powers from foreign lands to hold sway.

With his personal retainers, Alfred had departed the scene determined to capture Guthrum in the knowledge that if he failed then it would only be a matter of time before the Viking menace would be once again upon them. That afternoon as the late sun faded Alfred rode hard but never quite catching Guthrum and the mounted remnants of his army. He knew where they were headed. It was eleven or so miles to reach the defensive palisades the Vikings had built around Chippenham during their occupation. As dusk settled Guthrum rode through the earthen ramparts and once again the Vikings ensconced themselves in the little settlement safe for the moment from Alfred's rampaging pursuit.

As they gave chase the Anglo-Saxons came across fleeing men outside Chippenham, the remnants of the Viking army that had attempted to keep up with their vanquished leader in his flight. They could not be allowed to rejoin Guthrum and Alfred had them executed on the spot. His mind was now swirling from the events of the day, still the adrenaline stirring him on despite his exhaustion. He recalled the last time he had been to this place. It had been only five months or so since he had fled from Chippenham. He remembered as if yesterday that fateful night; the twelfth night after Christmas when he and Ellie had fled, many of the population with them scattering in different directions: some to the sea and on to Wales, some to the west and yes, some who had loyally stuck with him as he had hidden during those late winter months and taken refuge at Athelney.

The contrast between their fortunes then and now did not weigh on him. Alfred's mind was still focussed upon the job in hand; the victory to secure their freedom had not yet been sealed. He needed to complete the job rather to somehow hope that he had done enough and leave the rest to serendipity and vague promises to his people that all would be well. That may be the way of other lesser leaders but it was not Alfred's way. His resolve had got him this far. It was not about to leave him now.

They made camp outside the gates of Chippenham that evening and it was then that he gathered his most trusted lieutenants around him. As the rest of his army quickly followed on from Edington they would lay siege he told them, preventing the Vikings from escape. He ordered his men to seize anything including horses, cattle and food that might fall into the Viking hands. He looked at Edgar his trusted servant who had been with him throughout their great ordeal.

"Edgar, take men and erect barricades downriver. No fresh supplies must reach the settlement. Station guards by the Avon preventing any escape at night by boat." He noticed the gash along the man's arm where a Viking sword had slashed him. At least the arm was still intact unlike so many of his fellows. Alfred touched him on the shoulder. "Are you alright my friend?" he asked him.

Edgar nodded. Evidence of the day's momentous events were still etched upon his face. He smiled to his sovereign as Alfred spoke: a smile of exuberant joy, of sheer relief at what they had achieved. Alfred had inspired them and told them the job could and would be done. The most significant of battles upon which so much rested had been won. Whilst the final victory was not yet theirs the odds they knew were now heavily stacked in their favour.

In some strange way their exhaustion was the ultimate proof of what they had been through. Tomorrow they would as one tighten the siege still further as their victorious army joined them at the gates of the stronghold. Tomorrow and the next day and the day after that they would hold the siege. And then, when that siege was won Alfred unbeknownst to them would do the incredible!

Chapter 14

Autumn 2018

Onslow Ratcliffe stared ahead at the imposing building signifying its importance like Cleopatra's Palace, once one of the wonders of the ancient world before the tsunami had destroyed it fourteen hundred years ago. He looked up at the lines of flags flying as if in homage to its incumbents. No tsunami, no power on earth would destroy the EU project he mused.

Yes the Euro had proved a disaster for the Southern European countries several of which had barely recovered since the financial crisis ten years previously. A generation of young people had suffered unemployment on an unimaginable scale sacrificed upon the altar of the European project. Yes the regulatory burdens and requirements of officialdom had seen the EU share of global trade decline dramatically, whilst nation states had become restive as they had seen their sovereignty gently and quietly passed to their unelected masters in Brussels. It had given new meaning to the term salami sliced; the surreptitious and relentless transfer of powers that had so infuriated parties on the extremes that now featured prominently in the latest polls. But this was the EU building Onslow thought and the power that lay within its walls was formidable indeed.

It had been a rainy October morning but now the clouds had cleared allowing the sun to break through and cast a radiant glow over the scene. Beneath the great building smartly dressed EU bureaucrats walked purposefully through a myriad of revolving doors, others across the wide open paved areas all going about their business of managing the lives of the 500 million souls under their remit. When Onslow Ratcliffe walked into the main lobby he was one of many, knowing as he did never to look lost lest some unknown official challenged him. But Onslow had a reason to be there. He knew his way to the upper floors for his assignation.

He stepped into the lift and stood silently, observing the unspoken rules never to make eye contact with its occupants, never to move or show emotion, pretending almost to be nonexistent as it sped silently upwards. His mind flashed back to the last time he had found himself in a lift in Brussels - to Ingrid, to the way in which she had clutched him to her body, to the passionate way in which she had kissed him.

He had dressed as he invariably did in a smart navy suit, a dark tie, a white shirt and gold cufflinks handed down to him from his father. His suit was far from the most expensive. Never trust a man in an Armani suit he had been advised years ago. He had not forgotten the words yet there were plenty of Armani suits on display that day.

He alighted from the lift and looked down at the scene far below. Little dots, human beings like swarms of ants were moving hither and thither. He paused momentarily beside a glass panel and straightened his tie in the reflection. Then in the manner of the Prince of Wales he patted his jacket pocket, his displacement behaviours signifying a hint of anxiety to any connoisseur of body language that might have been looking on. He continued walking, striding along the marble corridor that stretched as far as he could see. As he kept his eyes straight ahead he saw the attractive woman in a jet black dress and matching heels walking towards him. Her waist was slim giving way to shapely hips and legs discreetly covered, but enticing nevertheless to any testosterone filled onlooker. Her short steps and heels accentuated the sway of her hips in the manner of a model but subtly also in the manner of a sophisticated woman, self confident and composed.

As they walked towards one another Onslow smiled as their eyes registered each other's presence. He had not expected to see Ingrid till later. She stopped as he approached. She put her hand on his but did not kiss him maintaining her business air in front of any who might have walked by. Her eyes were beautiful. Beautiful and spirited, eager to get to know him betraying the attraction she felt for him. She smiled and spoke in hushed tones as she held his arm.

"Onslow I did not expect to see you till later. You are on your way to Francois, I guess?" He nodded.

"Come to the usual place by the square later, say at 7.00," she said. There was an air of command in her voice just as before. Again Onslow nodded.

"I'll look forward to it," he replied. They instantly walked on each giving no hint of the chemistry between them. Neither looked back, each happy at the prospect of their evening tryst.

A minute later a secretary met Onlsow outside the palatial office of Francois Du Bain.

"Mr Ratcliffe, I presume?" she asked him. "We have been expecting you."

He acknowledged her and together they entered the hallowed ground. Francois Du Bain was seated behind his enormous desk in his high backed leather chair. He looked up and smiled and walked towards Ratcliffe his hands outstretched.

"Onslow how nice to see you again. How kind of you to come over to see me?" His tone was courteous in a friendly but formal way, just a hint of graciousness in his choice of words as if in another incarnation he could have been the Queen.

He placed his hands upon Onslow's shoulders and kissed him on both cheeks. Onslow Ratcliffe had grown used to the greeting but deep down felt uncomfortable retaining his English reserve. If it had been Ingrid kissing his face it would have been a different matter. He glanced across the office taking in the modern paintings each hung in perfect symmetry. The huge TV screen on the opposite wall was showing Sky news but the volume had been muted. Francois ushered him to sit and Onslow felt himself sink into one of the four sumptuous sofas that formed a square around the oversized marble table. For a second or two Francois stood over him before he spoke.

"I could offer you coffee, but I think we deserve something stronger don't you think?"

An ice bucket had been placed in the middle of the table containing a bottle of fine champagne. He poured two glasses and handed one to Onslow.

"Pol Roger, I see," pronounced Onslow. "Churchill's favourite champagne!"

"Ah, your Winston Churchill," Francois replied. "He stood up against those who threatened our freedom. I respect your Mr Churchill of course."

The supreme irony of his words were missed by Onslow but they raised their glasses and toasted the great man. Onslow waited for Du Bain to raise the issues for their discussion as he wished.

"Ingrid has told me you kindly gave her the confirmation she asked for concerning one or two issues that are important to us." He reiterated each of the issues she had got Onslow to concede upon. "I want to thank you for such a constructive approach, agreeing to each as you did. I know that you value a good Withdrawal Agreement between us so your words of reassurance upon these matters will not go unrewarded I am sure."

Good for whom Onslow wondered. His words as always were carefully constructed; a subtle text of negotiating leverage wrapped in a charade of charm suggesting that in some perverted way it had been Onslow whose skills had brought the breakthrough.

"There are just a couple of other minor things I need you to confirm for me Onslow."

Onslow's mind registered the danger signals of what was to emanate from his lips. Minor for whom he wondered? He liked Francois though and had not forgotten his generous hospitality at their last meeting. However, he was astute enough to realise that nothing Francois Du Bain ever did was without purpose.

Francois took off his glasses and played with them as he spoke. "Last December your government conceded the Irish backstop so that we are agreed upon no infrastructure at the border or any related checks or controls away from the border. But your government has said no to a border in the Irish Sea since that would break your union. However my dear Onslow, you must understand that your union cannot be our main concern. The obvious answer is for the entire UK to remain within the customs union and single market accepting our laws and regulations. I am sure you will agree? You can call it by another name of course if that is helpful!"

Onslow knew the value to the EU of their significant December concession. It had been a catastrophic mistake as far as the Brexiteers were concerned. As he had discussed with Sir Stephen, it had disingenuously been a concession calculated to allow the EU to force Britain into accepting the softest of Brexits since a hard border between Britain and Northern Ireland could never be accepted.

"I am sure we can find a way forward that is satisfactory to you," Onslow said.

Francois smiled and raised his glass. "I am so glad to hear that. I should add also how pleased we are that so many of your ex Prime Ministers and well known politicians, men of authority whom we respect, have been coming across on Eurostar every week to reassure us to hold our nerve. They say that if we do so, the British people will come to their senses and Parliament will vote to extend Article 50 and have a second referendum. Your Remainers have been so helpful to us Onslow. We are only doing as they have asked. You do understand that don't you?"

Onslow knew that to many of the Brexiteers these senior politicians had been deemed fifth columnists, the collaborators, the men of Vichy, but to the British establishment they had been invaluable in keeping Britain tied to the EU. The referendum result was being systematically emasculated he knew but what mattered was staying aligned to the EU in all but name. He looked at Francois thoughtfully.

"At the end of the day we are all on the same side, need I say more?" Onslow declared. Francois gave another smile of satisfaction.

"You have asked Ingrid that we will be, how shall I say, discreet, not revealing to the British press those concessions to which you have kindly agreed. I would like to reassure you my dear Onslow that this is precisely what we will do for you and without asking anything from you in return! The things we have asked for and the things as you know we shall be asking for after the transition period will be done without fuss, hidden away in the small print you understand." His voice came sincerely as if to emphasise the point.

"I will communicate that to my colleagues," Onslow reassured him. "I know they will be grateful to you."

Both men drank from their glasses and immediately Francois refilled them. He settled himself, leaning back in the sofa and crossed his legs. "Of course," he uttered, "of course time is running out for us – if that is you British want to reach a deal before our November summit. There is really no time left. But I have a proposal Onslow, a proposal that I am sure you will agree is a sensible way forward, sensible of course for both of us."

His words came with an ingratiating smile before proceeding. Onslow waited for what was to come.

"I would like you to bring your team here to Brussels next week for a meeting, just to confirm what we have agreed you understand. Then we will have the basis for the Withdrawal Agreement I think – the natural evolvement of your Chequers offer."

Onslow consented, agreeing to alert the British team. Their business had been concluded and while he knew

Francois had got everything from him he wanted, he knew also he was essentially doing what his Downing Street masters wanted. An agreement would be reached even if the British red lines stated so confidently at Lancaster House had long ago been rendered redundant.

The Pol Roger had been emptied and both men stood and embraced. Francois put his hands upon Onslow's shoulders just as he had at the start of their meeting.

"We must go to my club again my dear friend, as we did before and the drinks will be on me," he declared. He rubbed his hands through his grey, greasy hair.

"I like you Onslow. You are a pleasure to do business with."

Two hours later the lights had come on at the bars around the square nearby. A pleasant atmosphere pervaded the place frequented as it was by happy drinkers at the end of the working day. Many were members of the army of European officials who so dominated the area. They had pushed up the employment costs for local companies competing for secretaries and administrative personnel. Many had sought employment at the Commission eager to partake in the bounty it had prescribed to itself. But the local bars and restaurants had thrived benefitting from lucrative salaries and expense accounts. And it was at one such bar as previously that Onslow Ratcliffe now found himself seated as Ingrid approached.

He stood and embraced her. Immediately he felt her respond gripping her hands around his back and holding him tightly to her. She kissed him and let her lips linger on his before pulling away. She was still dressed as he had seen her earlier in an alluring black dress that clung voraciously to her body tantalisingly reflecting the contours of her figure.

They ordered champagne and as they talked she crossed her legs slowly and dangled one shoe, letting it hang provocatively from her naked heel just as she had at their previous encounter.

Afterwards they strolled arm in arm to a discreet restaurant, one of many frequented by her. The waiter recognised her and gave a deferential nod of recognition. He showed them to a table covered with a perfectly ironed damask cloth, shiny cutlery and the tallest wine glasses that had become the fashion. There was something different Onslow noticed to their previous assignation. This time Ingrid never once raised the subject of their negotiations. They talked of each other. She was half French Ingrid told him. Her grandfather had been one of the 350,000 members of the Resistance she said, clearly proud of her family history. He had been executed by the Germans on D Day. As she spoke it was the only moment Onslow saw her poise falter.

She had followed in the footsteps of her father and joined the Commission following her graduation. She had never married but had submerged herself in her career and in the social life that emanated from it. It was only at the end of their dinner that she brought up the negotiation.

"Francois told me he has invited your negotiating team to come to Brussels shortly." He nodded as she took his hand in hers. "Francois is very charming but he knows what he wants. I hope you will be able to persuade your British colleagues to be generous to his demands Onslow. It would be good to get a Withdrawal Agreement sealed before the November summit."

Ingrid's words struck home to Onslow, earnest and well meaning but also containing a hidden agenda designed to manage his expectations. He knew how badly they wanted the British to hand over the promised £39 billion, but it was a leverage Downing Street had been unwilling to exert. She didn't wait for his response.

"Come on," she said, "My flat is nearby, come and spend the night with me." Her voice with its sexy accent was confident, knowing he would not decline the offer. She leant across the table and kissed him as if to seal his unspoken agreement. The candle cast a glow upon her skin Onslow noticed, illuminating her sun tanned flesh, still young and toned, unlined and inviting him to touch her. He gazed into her eyes and she reciprocated, a sensual smile spreading across her lips.

She led him from the table and to her apartment. It was one of many she told him financed by the Commission and luxuriously laid out. She held him by the hand and led him directly into the bedroom. Only a lamp lit the room lending it a romantic air. She kept her back to him as she disrobed in a second like an actress who had practised the move many times. Now naked she turned and faced him. She stood provocatively and cupped both her breasts in her hands.

"Make love to me Onslow," she commanded him.

* * *

When Maggie alighted from the tube at Sloane Square station she glanced up at the clear early evening sky. It was good to be above ground again. She took a deep breath of fresh air wishing she could somehow exhale all the stale air from the claustrophobic tube ride. No sooner had she walked the few steps to the Royal Court Theatre, she spotted Oscar pacing up and down on the pavement. She glanced quickly at her watch noting that she was not late.

As he saw her coming he gave her a warm and genuine smile. She liked this man she thought. There seemed a tender touch to him that she had been slow to fathom at Stella's supper party. She looked him up and down noting the same blue suede shoes, the swept back hair and the warm eyes.

"I am so pleased you could make it Maggie," he said. Instantly she detected the West Country accent that she had noticed before. It was not unattractive to her.

In a few minutes they had taken their seats all the while exchanging easy conversation. If she had had her reservations about what he might ask her, she began now to feel curiously at ease with Oscar. Never once did he mention his work or indeed enquire about hers. Instead they talked about their mutual interest in the current round of west end theatre productions. Maggie had seen several and kept abreast of the reviews.

They enjoyed the play and as they walked away a little later she wondered if that would be the end of their pleasant evening together. Reading her thoughts Oscar turned to her.

"I know a little pub close by Maggie. Would you like a drink? It seems too early to go home." She gazed into his warm eyes for the first time taking a moment to study them, letting her stare linger for just a moment longer than she intended. He reciprocated with a smile.

"That sounds nice," she said and let him lead her by the arm across Sloane Square. Chatting all the way they strolled past Peter Jones and into the King's Road. They found his intended pub. It was full of mainly young people; some still in suits from the day, others casually dressed noisily engaged in friendly banter. They sat together and drank and chatted.

"I love your accent, Oscar. Where do you come from?" she asked him.

He took his eyes off her and then looked back registering her interest.

"Devon, I was brought up on the edge of Dartmoor, not far from Plymouth. Did you know that Drake was a mayor of Plymouth? He built the leat system to bring fresh water to it."

Maggie smiled at his revelation excited at their mutual interest in history. She had studied Drake as she now studied Alfred. She had visited the old town of Cadiz. Whilst there she had stood at the harbour mouth and imagined Drake entering with his twenty four ships in that April of 1587, a year before the Armada had sailed. She had pictured him remaining fearlessly overnight, inflicting his damage upon the Spanish vessels preparing for the great invasion. Singeing the king of Spain's beard had become the stuff of legends but the story was true enough.

Inevitably their conversation turned to their work. He confirmed what he had indicated at Stella's supper: that he was the political columnist for a well known newspaper. As Oscar spoke his tone became more serious. He recalled her comments that evening, her obvious reluctance to speak of the Brexit negotiations.

"Maggie, I want you to know that I will not try to pry into your work just because I write a political column. I actually asked you out because I was attracted to you, for no other reason I assure you."

For the first time she touched his hand, suddenly reassured at this remark. It seemed unusually explicit. The attraction was certainly mutual she could not deny it. She looked at his lovely eyes convinced he was sincere.

"Thank you for respecting my position. It is very difficult for me Oscar, there are tremendous pressures. I am in a senior role. I know a lot and much of it would be a revelation. Sometimes I am tempted to spill the beans but I really am not sure."

He detected the anxiety in her voice. Now it was he who took hold of Maggie's hand.

"You are not the only one to be worried Maggie. There are 17.4 million people who voted to leave and who believed the Prime Minister's repeated confirmation that we would take back control over our laws, our borders and our money. But as you know better than I, that is a pretence by Downing Street."

Oscar paused. She noticed the look of deep thought etched upon his face as he continued.

"Nearly a hundred years ago Britain agreed it would no longer make laws that controlled the lives of the people of Australia. Now any Australian would feel outraged at such a thing. Yet Downing Street is actually proposing we ourselves accept that – signing up to effectively becoming a colony of Europe. No wonder the people are getting restless and any outburst by you or others like you could ignite real sparks of protest. We know what is going on Maggie and it is getting ugly."

For a moment there was silence between them as she pondered his words. Before she could speak Oscar continued: "Let me just say this. When politicians speak out it carries weight. But when a civil servant speaks out from the inside then it is dynamite. If you revealed that what is going on is essentially a betrayal and I gave it the oxygen of publicity, all hell would break loose. You have my number Maggie. Come to me at any time, but I will not push you I promise."

Chapter 15

May 878

King Alfred, the victor of Edington, the inspiration of his people, stood outside the gates of Chippenham. It was a cool spring morning, the fourteenth day of the siege during which he had allowed no food or provisions of any sort to reach the decimated remnants of Guthrum's army. The siege had been made water tight as his forces fresh from their victory at Edington had followed Alfred to Chippenham. In addition, barricades had been secured upon the River Avon preventing any supplies from reaching the besieged Vikings and any chance of escape by night.

Inside the settlement Guthrum had sat it out hoping somehow that Alfred, his men eager to return to their homesteads, would move on. But not for the first time he had underestimated his nemesis. Alfred had faced down the Viking leader – his victory would be secured.

It was upon this day that Guthrum, starved for food realised the time had come. It was a moment he had not for one single minute contemplated would ever arise. It represented the antithesis of everything he had been so confident of achieving. The tables had been completely and utterly turned by Alfred. And it was Guthrum, the once mighty Viking leader who now opened the gates to attempt a negotiation with the great Anglo-Saxon King.

As the significance of their victory now at last sank in, great waves of jubilation spread across Alfred's followers and then by word of mouth to his people – from Cornwall to Canterbury, from Wareham to Windsor, from Lyme Regis to London right across the kingdom. The freedom Alfred had promised them had been won. His defiance, his resolve and his refusal to settle for defeatism and humiliation had turned the tide.

The ignominy of it for Guthrum was however over-whelming, matched only by the certainty that Alfred would now do what he himself would have done had their roles been reversed: namely, have him executed instantly. His only option would be to fight to the last man in a futile effort to save himself.

However, for Alfred this was not necessarily the right option. There was no doubt he could have secured the final victory and executed all of the remaining Vikings but that final fight would inevitably mean the death of yet more of his followers.

The death of Guthrum after all of their sacrifice would be their reward. Alfred after all was not only the victor of this great ordeal, the defining moment that had so illustriously turned around his darkest hour. He was also someone who on a personal basis had much to be avenged for. He had seen his countrymen mown down in abject slaughter; the toll it had taken upon his own father Ethelwulf; the horrors of the slaughtered hostages Guthrum had left as his trademark in the alley ways at Wareham; the monasteries destroyed and the plunder of numerous settlements across the kingdom.

His own brother Ethelred with whom he had fought side by side at their great victory at Ashdown had suffered and later died as a result of his ordeal.

Alfred remembered that time well. It had remained seared into his memory: that year of 871 now seven years ago, in which they had fought major battles near Basingstoke and Reading after re grouping their forces at Windsor. It had been a tumultuous year in which he and his elder brother had taken on the might of the Viking army with mixed success. All the while he had witnessed the supreme sacrifice of those who fought with him. He had every reason now to exact his revenge as Guthrum sought terms.

But what followed as he stood beside his advisors and councillors was to mark Alfred out as 'the Great', distinguishing him from other leaders from history as being truly exceptional. For driven by his Christian beliefs that since his boyhood had been the cornerstone to his life, he did the totally unexpected; indeed after all he had been through, something incredible. He offered Guthrum his life – and with it the chance to live in peace and dignity.

Jesus had exhorted his followers to forgive their enemies, to turn the other cheek, to love their fellow man and if Alfred's life was to be true to his Christian principles then he too would not be found wanting at the day of judgment.

However, Alfred was also calculating in the terms of the surrender he agreed. As he tried to explain to his councillors there were good reasons to act as he did. His aim was to bring a lasting peace, to create the circumstances which would bring the Viking menace to an end, at least until he had overhauled the Anglo-Saxon's effectiveness as a mobile, structured fighting army. Moreover, should he execute

Guthrum it would only be a matter of time before another leader took his place and another Viking army assembled to inflict havoc upon his people. Alfred's sagacious mind did not stop at only offering forgiveness to Guthrum. It would be accompanied by a carefully constructed strategy.

Firstly, relating to the matter of hostages. It was almost unknown within treaty terms not to exchange hostages as guarantors of obeyance, their lives being forfeited should the other party break the agreed terms. However, such was the extent of Alfred's victory, he would offer not a single hostage. Yet he himself would choose as many hostages as he wished and they would constitute the most high ranking officials from Guthrum's entourage.

Secondly, as part of the agreement, Guthrum would renounce his heathen antipathy to the Christian faith and would himself be baptised and become now a man of peace. Alfred knew that men's lives could be turned around in such a way. To him the opportunity to change Guthrum from a man of violence was something he felt compelled to take. After all it was consistent with the requirement of Matthew's Great Commission. Christ's commandment was to go out and preach the Good News. He would do as his Lord instructed.

In return Guthrum would be confirmed as a king, of East Anglia, and from it he would acquire wealth from the local landowners and traders. He would look up to Alfred as his overlord but in turn be treated with respect and become an ally of Wessex, foregoing any future ambitions to invade the kingdom ever again. If Alfred could turn Guthrum into an ally, a man with whom he could share a culture and love of this land, not to mention a religious faith then perhaps, just perhaps the peace would last.

There was of course a risk that all of this would prove worthless, that Guthrum would renege upon the agreement. Alfred had been betrayed by him before. He remembered their protracted negotiations at Wareham and at Exeter during that cold winter of 876. He recalled how on both occasions the Viking leader had broken his word. Whilst he knew him personally, had come face to face with him, he could only contemplate whether this time he would keep to their agreement. But it was a risk that Alfred believed to be a calculated one in which the balance lay with his instincts – and they were to prove right.

So it was that Alfred took Guthrum and twenty nine of his most senior warriors back to the scene of his darkest hour at Athelney. Three miles away at the little church at Aller, just three weeks after the end of the siege at Chippenham, each of the Vikings were baptised. Alfred's sincerity was profound: he gave himself the role of godfather to Guthrum and raised him from the font during the holy ceremony.

As if to cement the relationship, Guthrum was given the name of Ethelstan confirming his new Saxon credentials. That name was significant. It had been the name of Alfred's oldest brother who had reigned as king of Kent under their father's lordship. Together with his role as godfather, Alfred had successfully bound the Viking leader into the new order based upon mutual trust and intended by him as the start of a genuinely harmonious relationship.

After the ceremony Alfred was generous, showering gifts in celebration to the new Christian king. As was the custom the recipients of such gifts now accepted a subservient role to their benefactor accepting him as their overlord. A new relationship was being carefully nurtured by Alfred. However, the celebrations were not over yet for Alfred laid on generous feasting and hospitality over the following weeks at Wedmore where he had his royal estate. The hatred between the sworn enemies was being turned into friendship as they sat feasting at the long tables: a remarkable transformation was taking place. That year at Wedmore the peace between them was confirmed.

How easy and how tempting it would have been for Alfred to have simply executed his vanquished enemy. Yet he had chosen carefully a different path on which to travel; a path derived from his passionate Christian beliefs destined to turn man's inhumanity to man into something else, something that aspired to a higher calling.

Several months later in October of that year of 878, the Vikings left Chippenham and withdrew from Wessex spending time at Cirencester before withdrawing in 879 to East Anglia. During that period another Viking fleet had sailed up the Thames as far as Fulham. Guthrum or Ethelstan as he was now, chose not to join them and kept to his new accord with Alfred. Seeing the forces of Alfred in Wessex and Ethelstan in East Anglia, the fleet sailed from London to launch instead an onslaught upon swathes of Belgium and northern France.

Over the coming years Alfred's strategy kept the peace and the dreams he had shared with Ellie were turned into reality. He built longships able to give at least a modicum of defence at sea. He reorganised the military hubs across the kingdom with a standing army ready and able to defend against future aggressors. He strengthened the judicial system acting as judge and arbiter to enforce just laws.

But Alfred was above all keen to ensure his people were

given the foundations for a Christian life. He translated part of the book of Psalms which for him amounted almost to a biography. Many had been written by David representing his despair and his trust in God turning that despair into triumph over his enemies. To Alfred they mirrored his own life and like so many others down the ages he took inspiration from them. The church would be supported and the people taught to practise the moral code that he himself had tried to live by.

King Alfred died on the 26th day of October 899 at the age of fifty. He had reigned for twenty eight and a half years. His legacy was to pass down the generations, to be respected and admired by all those who value their freedom. In his final years he and his sons to follow had inflicted defeats again upon the Vikings after Ethelstan's death. Indeed the Vikings would be defeated in London and elsewhere and in the decades after his death Alfred's sons would go on to liberate much of England from the Viking menace.

But the foundation to that success could not be denied. Alfred's vision, his resolve and his inspirational leadership to win for his people the supreme gift of freedom, sprang from those days of defiance in the swampy marshes of Athelney – truly Alfred the Great's darkest hour.

Autumn 2018

Maggie Taylor finally put the book down. The 2.00 o'clock meeting Sir Stephen had called now beckoned and without further delay she needed to go. As she had gobbled down her sandwich, her office door closed to repel intruders, she had used the quiet time to complete Alfred's story. His persever-ance, his inspirational leadership, his triumph in the teeth of adversity matched Churchill in every way she thought, as indeed the great man himself had admitted. As she closed the book she felt strangely empowered for what lay ahead. The meeting she knew would be a contrast to what she had read: not the positive determination to settle for nothing less than total success but instead the usual defeatism and the endless talk of the need for pragmatism and further conces-sion making. Just then the phone rang.

"Maggie, Crispin Urquart here. How are you?" came the voice.

"I'm fine." She hesitated before correcting herself. "Well not really if you must know Crispin. The meeting this after-noon will depress me I have no doubt."

"I know. I am barely on speaking terms with Dawkins. But did you know I've been left off the contributors to the report he is compiling for Downing Street?" Urquart sounded clearly annoyed. She attempted to reassure him.

"Yes I did actually. He is trying to paint the most positive picture I'm sure. But don't worry. I submitted a comprehen-sive report to him setting out our costly errors and propos-als as to how to redeem ourselves."

"Thank God. I'll see you there shortly." Urquart put the phone down.

An hour later Maggie walked purposefully into their con-ference room. After her outburst at the last meeting she was uncertain what reception she would receive. Onslow was the first to greet her. They had not seen each other for several days and over the phone he had sounded reticent to expound upon his recent trip to Brussels. He smiled and kissed her on the cheek. It was genuine enough, though Maggie was aware of the fine line between his rakish charm and something more authentic. Their relationship had never fully recovered since their latest disagreement and at this moment she felt uncertain where the future lay.

She looked around as the ten strong group entered one by one each uncertain of the intentions of their leader. The last to enter was Sir Stephen Dawkins. Whether it was intentional Maggie knew not but she had noted it all the same. She glanced across to Crispin Urquart who had seated himself directly opposite. She caught his eye and they exchanged the suggestion of a smile. She knew the warmth between them was genuine. She had not forgotten their lunch that day when he had taken her into his confidence and shared his misgivings. She remained pleased that despite the temptation, she had abided by his advice when meeting Oscar.

Dawkins called the meeting to order. Momentarily there was silence in the room as each sat upright waiting for him to set the tone. The position they now faced looked extraordinarily tense. Huge pressures, partly self made as a result of putting themselves into a corner with their endless concessions to the EU, now presented themselves. The Conservative Party Conference had not proved as dire for the Prime Minister as some had predicted. The calls to 'Chuck Chequers' however had risen to fever pitch. Nevertheless Downing Street had remained intransigent much to the anger of many who believed in respecting the people's will, not to mention the manifestos of both Conservative and Labour at the General Election.

Only that morning her most prominent tormentor had referred to Chequers as the biggest humiliation since Suez.

Maggie could not disagree. Her discussions with Stella concerning Chamberlain and Churchill; their clashes over appeasement and the deceit that was the Munich agreement had struck home. 'Peace for our time' then was the equivalent of the Prime Minister's insistence that the will of the people was being respected now.

Her perceptive mind had been on fire as she had fathomed through the various similarities. They had been many for sure: the naivety and impotence of the negotiation; the pressure from the whips to show loyalty no matter how much the leader had ignored the warnings; the pretence to the people of parity in air power to Germany then, and the pretence to the people that Britain would no longer be rule takers of the EU now. And then there was the assurance of our freedom to exercise our own regulations and free trade agreements which she knew on the present course was simply an illusion.

No agenda had been issued. Each sat still, the merest hint of apprehension written upon their faces. Sir Stephen Dawkins looked up and his eyes locked in upon each one of them in turn. His face was expressionless, not stern but reflecting the gravity of the situation in the calm unflappable way that was the civil service hallmark. He began to speak in a low monotone voice.

"The purpose of our meeting today is to prepare ourselves for the most important session yet with our Brussels counterparts which will take place at the European Commission next week. It is intended to seal the Withdrawal Agreement in line with the PM's wishes. As you know Downing Street is overseeing this and we are now bypassing any input from the Brexit Minister so the horseplay will be down to us. I will ask Onslow to bring us up to date with the situation following his most recent trip to Brussels which I gather was successful Onslow?"

Maggie's eyes darted around the table as Onslow Ratcliffe began to speak. Still the faces were expressionless. If anyone was surprised by the announcement of the Brussels meeting they were not showing it.

Onslow chose his words carefully.

"Thank you Sir Stephen. I have had a productive time in Brussels," he began. "Following our last meeting I can report that the EU has agreed to ensure no undue publicity is given to the various concessions to which we have agreed. The British press, even with their infinite capacity to be mischievous, will not be given access to the most sensitive areas. As everyone will understand this did entail my agreeing to various new undertakings as I have outlined in the report I have now circulated."

Maggie immediately looked at Crispin who read her thoughts. Neither had seen such a report. The admission given by Onslow in the most placid of tones took their breath away. Strangely everyone else in the room demonstrated no surprise whatever. Before she could say anything Dawkins spoke.

"I am sure each of you will join me in thanking Onslow for a job well done, no doubt stressful to him but carried out with the usual British stiff upper lip!" He allowed himself a self satisfied smile at this touch of ironic humour and everyone else smiled with him.

He continued. "As you know the EU insist upon Northern Ireland remaining effectively under the customs union abiding by rules promulgated by the EU. But a hard border down the Irish Sea will sever our union and the DUP won't stand for that. The answer is to keep Great Britain entirely within the customs union."

At this Maggie could no longer contain herself. She tried her hardest to couch her comments diplomatically.

"Sir Stephen, may I remind us that the only reason we are in this dire predicament is because on December 8th last year Downing Street made the catastrophic concession to the EU to accept the Irish backstop in the event of no deal. We have allowed the EU to either annex Northern Ireland for itself with no hard border or to break up the British union by virtue of a border in the sea. The answer is to withdraw that concession, not to make matters even worse by conceding the whole of the UK remaining within the customs union. That would be seen by the British people as tantamount to treachery. It would make a mockery of the referendum."

Maggie had not held back. Immediately the room broke into uproar with some of the esteemed attendees throwing decidedly ungentlemanly language in her direction. She glanced across to Crispin who nodded his agreement with her outburst. Sir Stephen looked sternly at Maggie, his face turning redder as he worked himself up.

"Downing Street would never be willing to lose face. We have to go along with it and manage the situation as best we can. Besides it might not be a bad thing in the eyes of many for the entire UK to remain tied within the EU!"

Maggie suddenly smelt a rat, her astute mind picking up the implication of his words.

"Are you suggesting that we were wilfully complicit in giving this concession Sir Stephen? Are you suggesting it has been purposefully given in order to keep Britain effectively within the EU, having to accept all their rules but without any say?"

She had planted a hand grenade in the room. Her eyes darted across the table, then for some reason to Onslow. She saw his smile, the look of guilt and admittance or was it embarrassment, to Sir Stephen. Immediately she knew her suspicions were confirmed. Following the concessions by Onslow and now this, she was suddenly furious as she waited for his response.

Sir Stephen Dawkins looked flummoxed. He was not used to being cross examined in this way. The argument continued for several minutes with Crispin Urquart now becoming involved in support of Maggie. Onslow chose to say nothing.

Eventually Dawkins moved the conversation on to their preparation for next week's meeting in Brussels.

"I have received from several of you the required report upon our current position for my submission to Downing Street. Here is a copy for each of you. My conclusions are at the back and we will use that as our basis in Brussels next week."

He handed a sheaf of formally written up notes across the table. It was a sizeable document representing Maggie's input in addition to that of selected colleagues. As soon as the meeting concluded she returned to her office and slammed the door, still angry at the revelations she had extracted. She threw the report down on her desk, feeling exhausted and depressed in equal measure.

The temptation to look inside the document was too much however. She picked it up and began to thumb through the pages. Quickly she found what she was looking for: her own contribution, the comprehensive setting out of the most salient points that she knew would raise eyebrows in Downing Street where so much of the blame for what had happened lay. She read quickly, glancing through what she had written.

As her eyes scanned the pages she suddenly erupted.

"Oh my God!" she cried.

It was a spontaneous outburst of fury. Each of her points of constructive criticism, the points that had been of the most crucial importance, had been carefully and assiduously redacted.

Chapter 16

Autumn 2018

Across Britain a few days later the tension over the Brexit negotiations had been ratcheted up as the news media had gone into overdrive. Every new headline had raised the temperature both with Remainer pressure groups determined to secure a second referendum and with the Brexiteers.

A rally by Remainers had claimed several hundred thousand supporters. Their protest may have achieved their objectives but as Maggie knew it had also undermined Britain's negotiating stance which still was not concluded. Not for the first time Brussels was further emboldened to hang out in the belief the British government would be compromised once again from within.

However, it was from the Brexiteers that real anger at what was happening had pervaded across England's green and pleasant land. The denial of democracy, of the promise to deliver whatever the referendum result would be, had roused the vitriol of many.

At the weekend a vociferous rally had been organised by one of the pressure groups determined to see the referendum result honoured. To noisy acclaim leading spokesmen had torn into the idea of Britain becoming trapped within

186

the customs union in a state of purgatory unable to assert her independence. An astute analyst had tweeted that the Prime Minister had promised no less than 21 times in the House of Commons that Britain would leave the customs union. And yet now with the latest revelations of keeping Britain shackled, at least one leading orator at the event had called the Prime Minister duplicitous. The atmosphere had been febrile. A march to London was underway and other pressure groups were acting in concert. Rallies were taking place in Birmingham, Harrogate, Bournemouth, Gateshead and Torquay.

So it was that as Maggie arrived at Sloane Square that Saturday morning to see Stella she noticed the news vendors making their offerings to passersby with unusual zeal. Two of the headlines had used the word 'BETRAYAL' in heavy capital letters. 'GOVERNMENT UNDER PRESSURE TO CHUCK CHEQUERS' ran another. Others had highlighted the imminent threat of more Cabinet resignations. Maggie walked on. She had no need to buy one. She knew far more of what was going on from the inside.

That morning she had woken to the 'Today' programme as she invariably did. Whilst the presenters in general had professionally masked their personal opinions one in particular to Maggie's keen ear had failed to do so; on several occasions the idea of a second referendum had been talked up with Remainer interviewees who seemed to be interrupted with far less alacrity. At least for now she had managed to put the latest such interview out of her mind. In any case the people had voted not only at the referendum on the issue but at the General Election at which the vast majority had supported the Labour and Conservative promises to properly expedite Brexit. If two national votes were not enough what possible legitimacy might a third vote have?

The walk to Cadogan Place did her good. She thought back to the walks she and Stella had undertaken during their visit to the Dordogne: the relaxed atmosphere between them as they had strode around the ancient bastide towns of Domme and Sarlat; their conversations over wine and French cooking at the little restaurants amidst the medieval stone arches at Monpazier. Stella had been a confidant to whom she could unleash her frustrations in absolute confidence and it was Stella again she now wished to see.

Twenty minutes later she found herself staring out over Cadogan Gardens as her friend made tea. They had changed since she had last set her eye upon them at the supper party. Now the first hints of autumn were on display; the first leaves lay upon the grass; the unstoppable, always reliable laws of nature asserting their power over man's environment. The merest hints of autumn gold were tantalisingly playing upon the eye of the onlooker raising expectations of the glorious colours to come yet holding back as if bringing on the tension.

But as they spoke it was the tension of what was to come elsewhere that occupied their conversation. Stella listened patiently as Maggie gave in to her need to confide to her friend. Downing Street she told her had given in relentlessly: the doubling of the so called divorce bill; the crippling Irish backstop that had caused the latest impasse; on the freedom to make trade deals; on the supremacy of the European Court of Justice, and so much more. Every concession had been readily swallowed up without exchange. All had been denied of course. But as Kipling had stated 'The end of that game is oppression and shame, and the nation that plays it is lost.'

Stella put down her tea and rested her hand on Maggie's. Never had she heard her old friend sound so depressed. Ever since she had known her, Maggie had been positive, full of self confidence, clever and popular. She had radiated her love of music and history and her lovely unpretentious personality. Stella listened as Maggie continued.

"Up to recently I have enjoyed my work. But over the last few months I have come to realise that I am a party to a bungling negotiation that amounts to a deceit. I seem to be an accomplice to what is going on."

Stella nodded. "The government had the biggest mandate in British history Maggie to bring back our independence. I read that around 3.5 million more people gave their support to Brexit than to any party at any General Election, ever!"

"An appalling election campaign didn't help!" she replied. "Do you know Stella, I truly believe this is the worst government since Heath. He made false promises over sovereignty too, you know. You told me that Churchill had been taught to believe in the democratic will of the people and to trust them. That is not what is happening now. Trust is going out of the window and millions are feeling betrayed. There are marches already. The Conservatives will be out of power for decades."

Stella stood and gazed out of the window. "You can always go to Oscar," she declared.

"I know. He dated me and took me to the theatre, here at The Royal Court. He was utterly refreshing Stella. A genuinely nice guy and it was so tempting to give him my story."

"Well, perhaps you should," Stella opined, speaking slowly.

"Unlike many of the politicians who put loyalty to Downing Street and party above everything, you are more principled. Perhaps you should talk to him."

Maggie stared at her friend but said nothing.

"Remember the words of Churchill, Maggie. He and his supporters were a tiny minority in Parliament when he bravely stood up to Chamberlain. Remember his words, 'Thou art weighed in the balance and found wanting.' You are as brave Maggie, I know you are. Speak to Oscar. Speak to him and speak to those who will give your revelations the oxygen of publicity – just as Churchill did."

* * *

As Maggie Taylor and her colleagues had dined together at their hotel in Brussels a few days later, one person had been missing. Onslow Ratcliffe had made his excuse and she had slept alone. But as their relationship had deteriorated it hadn't worried her unduly, as it might have two months earlier. When they met as a group in the central lobby at the EU Commission she did not mention it and they embraced as if the matter was of no consequence.

Maggie looked up at the high roof, the imposing staircase, the glass lifts speeding their occupants to their destinations. It presented all the hallmarks of the all powerful Mecca to the European Project. She had been to the Reichstag in Berlin, the dome of which had been designed by Norman Foster as a symbol of the reunification of Germany. Somehow the EU building made a different statement she thought, not of unification but of an arrogant assumption of its own power. The dome symbolised more importantly that the people are above the government. The irony with the anti democratic tendencies at the EU and what was now happening in Britain was not lost on her.

Two political advisors on the express orders of Downing Street had arrived with Sir Stephen Dawkins. They wore an outward mask of confidence but Maggie read the body language registering the underlying tension. The group of twelve shook hands like Wimbledon doubles partners observing their ritual, obsessively touching hands after every shot as if to impart mutual encouragement. The poignant moment in history of the last supper flashed through Maggie's quick mind. The disciples there had numbered twelve as well. She wondered if like Christ's momentous announcement to them, there would be a momentous conclusion to their meeting also.

The British contingent, now all present, were shepherded to the upper floors and into their appointed conference room to wait in tense anticipation for their adversaries. It was laid out in the boardroom style, a long thin table down the room. On each side twelve jotters had been laid out with accompanying crystal glasses with the precision that would have been ascribed to a country house dinner party. Cold bottles of water were spread evenly between little vases of highest grade Belgian chocolates designed to subliminally and subtly confirm they were in the hands of their hosts and masters to whom it was implicit the concessions would flow, even before a word had been uttered.

Maggie noticed the formally written name cards that had been pre arranged setting out their seating positions. High backed luxury executive chairs lined each side. The Europeans were to be seated abreast looking outwards at the window, each one facing directly their opposite number. Thoughts of Alfred flashed through her mind; his brave men doing likewise as their shields had interlocked determined to secure their freedom as were the British now. Somehow she knew today they would achieve but a shadow of Alfred's glory.

The British contingent was to be seated with their backs to the window, below which radiators had been deliberately left on. The detail had escaped Maggie. The British would feel the heat as time went on, quite literally. Neither had she detected that each of the British height adjustable seats had been set at precisely 4 centimetres below the height of their European counterparts, not enough to be noticed but subconsciously able to have the desired effect. The room was well lit made so by spotlights high above the European side pointing at the eyes of their British counterparts.

Maggie Taylor had been to the EU Commission building before for previous meetings but when their adversaries strode in she recognised no one. Each shook hands with everybody else. She had been trained as part of her negotiation tutorage to watch the body language. Instantly she noted the dominant handshakes, the right hands of their European adversaries turned into a closed position indicating their dominance; the firm grip, the extended other hand touching the back of her shoulder. She had been trained by her coach at Lawrence Lemmy back in London just how to respond and as each handshake was given she reacted accordingly.

She looked across the table. The urbane Francois Du Bain had seated himself in the middle. At one side sat a sophisticated looking blonde haired delegate dressed in an elegant black dress who she noticed whispered in his ear at regular intervals. Maggie watched as she smiled across the table to her opposite number on the British side. It was Onslow Ratcliffe. They seemed to know each other she noticed. For just a brief moment the thought of Onslow's extra nights in Brussels occurred to her as she watched the eye contact between them. At the end sat Crispin Urquart drumming his finger nails upon the table. He caught Maggie's eye and smiled a smile of encouragement. Sir Stephen was placed next to the senior Downing Street aide directly opposite Ingrid. They seemed to be exchanging comments inaudible to anybody else.

It was Du Bain who opened the proceedings setting out what they hoped to achieve. All wanted a deal Maggie knew. The EU was keen above everything to secure the British offer of £39 billion with more to follow, dangling the prospect of a free trade deal at some unspecified future date. The irony was the benefit to them would be of greater significance than for the U.K., a double win in prospect; a jackpot to beat all others. However, on top the EU were determined to either lock Britain into a near permanent customs union or to annex Northern Ireland as they took advantage of the pitiful British concession to adhere to the backstop.

In all it was a terrible deal Maggie knew that was now taking shape. Before she had left London she had seen the double-decker bus with its incitement to 'Chuck Chequers'. She had seen too the latest wave of vociferous protesters in Westminster angrily denouncing it as a betrayal. She had heard the German Europe Minister calling for the Prime Minister to be constructive. She knew full well his meaning: to concede still further.

And so it was that as the next few hours moved inexorably on, the two sides remained engaged considering the options for an agreement. Who would give way first Maggie wondered? Even at this late stage the British could have exerted their leverage threatening to slash Corporation tax; to eschew the regulatory framework that had restricted their competitiveness; to enter into a Trans Atlantic trade agreement; to forget all talk of the £39 billion; to exert tariffs upon everything from French wine to German cars. Yet abiding by Downing Street's edict, she suspected they were about to fly the white flag, fecklessly and supinely giving way, the roar of the lion turning into a submissive whimper.

She said little, leaving as she had been asked the talking to Dawkins. But she could tell they were moving towards the final climax of this tragic symphony. Du Bain began to speak in a slow, deep, uncompromising tone.

"If you agree to having no unilateral right to pull out of the customs union and the single market – our laws, our regulations, our jurisdiction – then we will agree to this document being the basis of a Withdrawal Agreement for your Prime Minister to sell to the British Parliament." In the consummate skill of a trained negotiator it was said as a statement rather than a question.

Immediately Du Bain had issued the words he remained silent and for nearly a minute a pin could have been heard dropping in the room as Maggie held her breath. All the while Francois Du Bain fixed Dawkins with his stare, his expression set in stone, his chin jutting forward.

Maggie remained focussed gritting her teeth yet distracted also: distracted by thoughts of who would blink first; thoughts of the Viking Army finally being forced under

Alfred's onslaught to yield; thoughts of Alfred's refusal to succumb which had won the day and secured their freedom. They were days away from the anniversaries of Trafalgar, Agincourt and El Alamein. Why was it she wondered, that so many great British victories had been won on almost this exact day? Would this be one also?

The face of Sir Stephen Dawkins was now bright red, his forehead covered in perspiration which glistened around his temples as the spotlights had their effect. As Maggie watched intently, she saw him look at his political advisor, a fervent Remainer she knew, sat next to him. It was a look of compliant deference to the man who on the orders of the Prime Minister would sanction such a momentous humiliation. She held her breath, the tension in the silent room almost unbearable, all eyes upon the central characters in this great unfolding drama. Whoever broke the silence first she knew would in all likelihood give way. Then she saw the two men give the merest hint of a nod to each other. The body language said it all. A look of acquiescence and servitude was written upon their faces. Only when Dawkins then conceded did Du Bain allow a smile to emerge from his uncompromising features.

The inevitable that Maggie had so perceptively imagined had come quickly. This was no Trafalgar or Agincourt, no glorious victory as at Edington. The British side confirmed their assent in principle to the varied EU demands, the most costly of which were the enormous cash sums that would continue to be handed over, the Eurogeld that Alfred had refused, as Maggie had referred to it. Britain would remain under regulations imposed by Brussels and enforced by the ECJ. In effect Britain, the country that with a quarter of the globe as its friends across the Commonwealth had led the liberation of Europe in winning two world wars – not to mention the liberation from Napoleon a century earlier – would now assume the status of a colony of Europe; a vassal state, a rule taker without the freedom to negotiate the global trade deals that had been on offer.

The agreement was only in principle. Yet it formed the basis for the Withdrawal Agreement to be sold disingenuously by Downing Street and presented to Parliament for approval. However, it had been an abject capitulation on Britain's part. Newspapers had reported that the German official Martin Selmayr, the principal Brussels bureaucrat who revelled in the nickname the 'Monster of Brussels', had ordered that Britain be punished and pay a high price and that price would mean Northern Ireland effectively remaining within the EU regulatory regime. In so doing he had put the union at risk. Not only that, but Britain had allowed herself to be locked into the customs union without the ability to exert her independence, unless the EU gave its consent. Downing Street's promised freedom to enact trade deals around the world lay in ruins. It had been the greatest capitulation in centuries and to Maggie it was beyond belief that a British Prime Minister could now pretend this was somehow consistent with the referendum vote. The cost and the humiliation of Britain succumbing to the EU's bullying had been staggering.

As she left the conference room, a disgusted Maggie Taylor recalled the German industrial leader months before issuing his chilling words that Germany expected nothing less than total surrender from the British. Well, he had got his way alright, made possible only by Downing Street's collusion with her civil servant colleagues culminating in today's debacle. The fury of Brexiteers would be unbridled. But most of the British concessions would of course be disingenuously referred to at the forthcoming press conference as a win-win, a successful 'negotiation' that would paint the Prime Minister in the most positive light. Yet the truth was it was anything but; a national humiliation; a surrender that represented a travesty of what the people had voted for and been promised. And to Maggie's eternal shame her integrity had been compromised; she had been a party to it, a participant and accomplice to the ineptitude and deceit that over many months had now culminated in this debacle.

That evening she felt the need for a long, long walk, alone with her thoughts and without distraction. When she had spotted her colleagues, strangely including Ingrid and Onslow laughing and drinking just off the Grand Place, she had walked by unseen on the other side. As they had wined and dined thankful their ordeal was over, Maggie Taylor walked on through the central streets of the Belgian capital. She found the one place she could find peace from her travails. She walked into the great cathedral finding herself alone save for a few late tourists clicking their cameras some way from her. She looked up and noted the wonderful stain glass windows, seeking inspiration and solace from them. Half way along she sat down and sensed the weight lift off her shoulders.

Maggie had never been a Christian. Never that was until a barrister friend had persuaded her to do the Alpha Course. She had, at first reluctantly, become one of the 25 million across 170 or so countries to listen to the modules. The evidence had been compelling and since, she had read

197

'God's Undertaker' by the great mathematics professor, John Lennox. In it he had cited the conclusions of several Nobel Prize winners as to the existence of something beyond the process of mere evolution.

Allied to this her moral values had too evolved. Whilst friends had judged their life's achievement by how much money they could amass, how many properties they could own or how many countries they could tick off their bucket list, Maggie had taken a different view. To her, life was part of a significant journey and as such needed to have a meaning, given a value, a purpose so that at her own day of judgement she would be found to have used her life well. She had remembered a phrase from a service she had attended: 'Our souls and bodies to be a living sacrifice in the service of Christ'. What she might do now to uphold those values as she reflected upon her participation in the day's events now weighed heavily upon her.

As she walked to her hotel she felt an overwhelming feeling of shame.

Chapter 17

Three days had passed since Maggie's return from Brussels. During that time she had twice picked up the phone to call Oscar, twice putting it down half hoping, half convincing herself that somehow things would change. Perhaps the so called negotiation in Brussels culminating in Britain's abject capitulation and acceptance of the basis of the Withdrawal Agreement would turn out to be nothing more than a terrible dream from which she would emerge. But she knew the stark reality was anything but a dream and Stella's words inveighing her to do her duty ran true. The moral code running deep within Maggie Taylor's psyche was now overwhelming her like a river in flood compelling her, imploring her to call Oscar without further delay. No longer could she hold it back even if she wanted to. It was a force borne out of her innate integrity nourished and nurtured since as a child she had sat on her father's knee and gleaned her first inkling of right and wrong. Duty in the end was more important than safeguarding one's career.

At the start of WW2 several brave Tory members had done just that as they had come to realise their loyalty to Chamberlain had been so misplaced. Loyalty to the country in the end was more important than loyalty to Downing Street or to the likes of Sir Stephen Dawkins. Sitting in her flat she again picked up the phone and when Oscar agreed to come straight round she stood and gazed out of the window feeling a curious sense of relief as if a great and tumultuous weight had been thrown off her shoulders. Tonight she would sleep knowing she had had the moral fibre to do the right thing.

When he found his way to the flat she noticed Oscar's demeanour. It was kindly and concerned, not the hardened reporter she had supposed many in his profession to be. Clearly he knew just how difficult this was for Maggie. Perhaps it was helped by the attraction he felt for her, a genuine attraction initiated at Stella's supper party but like the making of fine sherry, gently added to and nourished at their date at the theatre. That evening he had parted with no more than a kiss to her cheek, their relationship if it could indeed be called such, had been barely embryonic. No hint of love at first sight. Rather a certain slow burning mutual attraction that given time who knows, like the first paint strokes on a canvas might magically evolve into a priceless picture.

They sat together and over coffee Maggie unburdened herself to him. She recounted the myriad of negotiating flaws that had at the stroke of a pen been redacted by Dawkins. She disclosed the endless list of concessions, the enormous cash transfers that had been agreed and her belief that no sooner had the Withdrawal Agreement been ratified and the cash transferred, Britain would be told it needed to accept other EU stipulations; the overarching authority of the European Court of Justice; being bound by the customs union perhaps called by another name, and a host of other demands as well.

On top of this she expanded upon the transition and the

optional extension, during which Britain would be a vassal state, for the first time in a thousand years ruled by others with no say whatever. And for this privilege we would pay up to £20billion. It would take longer for Britain to extricate itself from the EU than it did to win the Second World War.

In addition she gave to Oscar the inside story of the catastrophic concession on the Irish backstop that had passed so much leverage to Brussels in Britain's cringing capitulation. She expanded upon how the infamous agreement in December had been confirmed in writing in March and the resulting impasse that had turned Brexit into little more than a charade. It had been a litany of errors driven by Downing Street. Strangely it had been her study of Alfred, his incomparable characteristics of vision and leadership not to mention the lessons from Churchill too, that had helped her see the light.

As Oscar listened carefully, Maggie felt herself giving vent to all that she had witnessed. Northern Ireland she explained would actually be tied to even more stringent terms than the rest of the United Kingdom putting it under the auspices of the EU. 'United' the kingdom would hardly be! Shockingly too, unlike any normal contractual agreement, Britain would be unable to unilaterally withdraw, denied her sovereign right to jettison the customs backstop and seek her own tariffs and regulations without EU consent. The Withdrawal Agreement would actually lock Britain into a vassal state status and the key would be firmly in the pocket of its Brussels masters.

Brussels she told him had been left partying at the totality of their victory. In their view their tactics of conceding almost nothing might now pay off giving succour to the anti-democratic forces in Britain to push even harder for a rerun of the referendum. The surrender she told him had broken the explicit promises of that referendum, the manifestos of both major parties and Downing Street's own red lines as well.

No doubt she pointed out Downing Street would carefully choreograph a final agreement as a success for Britain condemning any who voted against it as being responsible for the consequences. Yet it was Downing Street and Downing Street alone who had led the country to the Gates of Hades. One thing she knew however. The matter would remain unresolved. One day she opined, a true leader would rise as Alfred had all those years ago and give Britain what it had voted for.

When Oscar left he did so as he had come. He gave her a kiss on the cheek. He looked her in the eye as if to reassure her that despite what he was about to print she was doing the right thing. A certain touch of empathy such as she had never experienced from Onslow Ratcliffe lay in this man's character. Perhaps when this was all over she told herself she would see this man again. As he walked out of the door she couldn't help feeling he felt the same way towards her. How strange she thought as she watched him from her window walking away, that in her own darkest hour she had found a tiny touch of happiness as yet cocooned but like Alfred's dream perhaps just perhaps, ready to be turned into reality.

Two days later Maggie stood again at her window and threw open the curtains. It was a clear blue sky somehow befitting for a Sunday morning she felt. She stretched her arms and looked across the road. The traffic of the week had abated as if dormant, waiting in suspense now for the new week to start. All seemed quiet on the western front today she thought. It was a strange feeling precipitant perhaps of the dramas to come once Oscar had gone to press. She thought of Alfred and his innate strength. Like her hero she would not be found wanting.

It was then that Maggie Taylor suddenly felt an overwhelming need to see her parents. She could not find clarity to her thoughts but something inside was urging her on to jump into her beloved Beetle and travel at once to Bournemouth to see them. To spend such a fine autumnal day beside the sea would perhaps raise her spirits. She rang her mother and confirmed she would be with them by noon and after a hurried breakfast set off.

As she sped down the M3 with the hood down she felt the wind rushing through her hair. It was cold to be sure but somehow reinvigorating as if cleansing her and rejuvenating her from all she had been through. She drove faster than usual allowing the sensation of speed and the wind upon her face to wash over her working their magic. The sun was bright though and that was what mattered. Every now and again she would allow herself a brief glance at the fields on either side. They looked beautiful under the clear sky, the definition of the trees crisp and clear in the morning sun. It was a day for walking she thought and being beside the sea with her parents would do her good.

Later when she pulled up she paused before going into the house. She looked at it admiringly taking in its handsome features. Her parents had downsized four years previously, and made it into their little sanctum. Inside her mother standing with open arms welcomed her and they hugged each other warmly. They had always been close. Maggie knew how fortunate she was to have been born with such a person as Jill Taylor as her mum. Sound, caring and without pretension, she had never shirked from giving Maggie all the support she could and when her daughter visited them she relished each occasion, invariably cooking up one of Maggie's favourite dishes.

"Where's Dad?" Maggie asked.

"He's reading I think, come through darling," her mother replied.

As Maggie entered the dining room her father looked up from the newspaper. As always on a Sunday he had bought two papers: a tabloid to lighten up the deeper reading of the broadsheet. Immediately he saw her, his profound mood lifted. He rose and embraced his daughter, his pleasure at seeing her suddenly written upon his face.

"Darling what a lovely surprise," he exclaimed. "Mum told me you'd called and were popping down for the day. How are you? Worn out I expect what with all your responsibilities."

"I'm okay," she replied. It was a bland enigmatic reply that masked her current state of mind. A look of concern shot across her father's face. "I'm okay really," she added in an effort to reassure him.

It was then she spotted the newspaper in which he had been immersed. She took in the headline and then the sudden realisation hit her. She was staring in disbelief at Oscar's double page article.

'BETRAYAL: CIVIL SERVANT REVEALS THE TRUTH BEHIND THE CHEQUERS DECEIT' ran the headline.

She snatched up the paper and immediately her eyes darted over the article. Everything she had disclosed to Oscar had been faithfully set down. Her father looked at her noticing her tense expression as her eyes read on.

"It's dynamite darling," he said. "It is truly shocking what has been going on. It makes a mockery of this country. Millions will be outraged. Democracy has been denied."

Maggie wondered what her father's reaction would be if she admitted to him she was the originator. He had always supported her. Throughout her 33 years she had never withheld secrets from him. She loved her dad. He had been her rock and role model. She knew she could confide in him and besides, right now she needed the love and support of her parents. She put her arms around her father and hugged him.

"Dad, can I tell you something?" she said gently.

David Taylor looked at his daughter sensing her need for a listener. He squeezed her hand lovingly encouraging her to open up.

"Dad this article came from me. What I have witnessed has been such a breach of trust that I had to act, to give the true story to a journalist. I just thank God we have at least to a degree, a free press still!"

She fell silent awaiting his response and for a moment her father looked away as he took in her revelation. Never would he have suspected Maggie as the source though he knew she was highly principled and had the guts to do the right thing. He still remembered the time when in her early career she had threatened to take a bad employer to an industrial tribunal if they didn't change their ways. She had been no quitter then when a matter of principle was at stake and if she had acted so again then it did not surprise him. He took her hands in his and looked her in the eye.

"Darling, I don't know what to say other than this." Maggie looked at him waiting for what was it come. "What the article contains is quite shocking, indeed outrageous. I am so proud of you for speaking out, so very proud my darling. Most people would not have the guts or worse still not have cared. You deserve a medal for doing so!"

As he hugged her tightly tears began to flow down Maggie's cheeks. Her father's approval meant everything to her. She had always wanted him to be so proud of her and in that she had never failed. His comfort was something she had not sought but when it had been freely and unconditionally given it hit her like a tsunami. The tears came pouring down and as they did her father clenched her to him. Just for a moment she thought of when she had sat seeking solace in the great cathedral at Brussels. Had not Christ too offered her unconditional love? Now her dear father was doing just the same. She clenched him to her as the tears flowed.

"Darling, let me tell you something," David Taylor's voice came calmly as if trying his best to hide his inner feelings. As Maggie took in her father's words she realised the conviction behind them: they were sentiments he had never shared with his daughter. "I was born into a great country, one that was proud of its history, proud of its hard won freedom. But I remember it as if it were yesterday; the time when Heath signed away our sovereignty, denying it of course. Brave democrats like Benn and Powell resisted but of course many Tory loyalists supported him just as they had before in supporting Chamberlain. Now history is simply repeating itself once again, darling. We are being led by a government which does not believe in respecting the people's will and is condemning us to servitude dressed up as a deep and special partnership."

He paused and glanced out of the window at a bird that had landed on the ledge. However, it was only a temporary distraction. He looked back at his daughter. "I was brought up darling in the post war generation to be rather proud of our nation – the country had led the world in so many ways in a dignified way. Under this Prime Minister those sentiments have been turned into feelings of being ashamed and humiliated. I just hope that one day a new leader will put backbone and hope into our country again as Thatcher did in the '80s."

David Taylor fell silent. He had said enough. He looked at his daughter intently and she saw the emotion in his eyes. A sudden and close feeling of empathy with her dad swept over her as if the generations had miraculously come together joined in unison by an inner value, a profound belief that could not be severed by date of birth; a conviction shared and valued, secured tightly within their genes, perhaps even since the days of Alfred she conjectured.

"But Daddy," she said sobbing. It was the first time she had called him that for a while. "But Daddy, I have been a part of it."

Maggie was crying now uncontrollably. She hugged her father tightly hoping in some way she could revive her strength from him. He clutched her to him and slowly, just slowly Maggie felt her strength returning.

One hour later her parents took her to their favourite hotel for lunch to cheer her spirits. It was set high above the Sandbanks spit affording a magnificent view of Brownsea Island. As they stood on the terrace with the sun shining over the scene she gazed across Poole Harbour.

The water was calm and the clear sky had lent it a translucent shimmering shade of blue. A ferry was ploughing its way serenely towards the harbour mouth. Her eye followed it as slowly it went out of view. She pictured the 120 Viking longships moored at Brownsea Island just as she had read in her book of Alfred: she imagined their intimidating presence upon the people of Poole who must have looked on in trepidation as Alfred had sought to hold the line at Wareham. The pages of the book came instantly back as she imagined too the fate of those longships: how they had been wrecked off Old Harry Rocks in that storm of 877. She hardly heard her mother call as their meal was served. She turned and felt the spell of Alfred's story suddenly lifting, her mind again turning back to today's reality.

Over a delicious lunch her parents attempted to cheer her but underneath Maggie's mood remained subdued. She tried her best to mask what was troubling her but when they returned to the house she immediately turned on the TV in search of the latest developments. She watched in horror at the BREAKING NEWS:

'A senior civil servant as yet unnamed has broken ranks by revealing the true extent of Britain's ignominious humiliation in the Brexit negotiations. It has outraged the Brexiteers and many more protesters are converging on London as the tension mounts.'

As she and her father watched the news coming through she felt his hand on hers as if giving her strength for what she knew would be the most testing time on her return. Downing Street and her civil service colleagues would be baying for her blood for sure.

When the time came for her to depart, Maggie looked lovingly at both her parents in turn. Her mother took in her pretty face framed by her lovely thick brown hair and for some reason she held her daughter more closely than ever before. Maggie turned then to her father, the man who had been the loving dad she could never have dreamt of having. She hugged him tightly feeling him clutching her to him. She turned away and drove up the road for some reason not daring to look back.

That evening back in Kensington Maggie poured herself a scotch and turned on the news. The headlines were alarming. Several of the Brexiteer rallies had formed into marches that were now converging upon London. Angry chants of "BETRAYAL" were beginning to resemble what she had feared; the people indeed were growing restive. As the reports of the latest meeting in Brussels had filtered through the media, the anger had been further ratcheted up aided and abetted now by her revelations. Principled Tory MPs were demanding a change – if not in the leader, at least in the policy. The voices of the 17.4 million people were demanding to be heard; demanding that the referendum result would be honoured as had been promised; demanding that the biggest vote in British history be respected.

Maggie watched entranced as cameras from helicopters zoomed in upon the protesters. These were not loud-mouthed rioters. These were the silent majority, roused from their apathy, their blood up intent upon making their voices heard. She thought for a moment of Alfred's call to the humble folk; to ordinary people, to rouse themselves to meet at Egbert's Stone to fight for their freedom, to rally in force to exert their will. These good folk were surely the equivalent of their noble forebears.

Banners filled the air. 'GIVE US OUR SOVEREIGNTY' proclaimed one. 'STOP THE SELL OUT' another. An effigy of the Prime Minister was hoisted high and EU flags with red lines daubed across and a host too of Union flags with the words FREEDOM adorned upon them.

Maggie switched the channel. The announcer with understated excitement in his voice announced the arrival in London of fresh groups from Torquay, Bournemouth, Peterborough and Essex; from the north too all converging from different directions; a great tsunami of human tide inexorably and intrepidly moving on the capital. Her furtive mind flashed again to Alfred; to the men and boys armed with no more than pitchforks and axes following the burning beacons set up by the reeves in answer to Alfred's call.

Outside her flat, Kensington Church Street had become peculiarly quiet. It occurred to her the residents were watching too, their eyes glued to the unfolding drama. There would be no protest here Maggie thought. This was establishment country, the leafy prosperous areas, the property owners who in Alfred's time would have paid the Danegeld happily and lived as lackeys to their Viking overlords.

She switched off the television. In order to sleep the last thing she needed at night was to sustain the stresses of the day. She thumbed through her motley collection of discs. As she sank beneath the sheets the tranquil sounds of Elgar's first symphony wafted through the flat. It was the sublime third movement, the one she knew had the power to transport her to another place.

* * *

It was at precisely 4.00 the phone rang in Maggie's office the next day.

"Maggie this is Sir Stephen. Would you step into my office

please?" His voice sounded stern. There was an uncompromising hint of antipathy in his tone.

"Yes of course, I'll be with you directly," Maggie replied.

She put the phone down and leant back in her chair. She had expected the call and now it had come. She stood upright and breathed deeply. She needed her usual confidence right now.

Less than five minutes later she knocked on Sir Stephen's door. She waited several seconds for the call to enter and when it came she walked in upright, her shoulders back. He did not look up and invited her to sit. Maggie said nothing and for a moment there was silence between them. He sat composed, his podgy hands pressed together, his face still and expressionless as if holding in his emotions. As ever he was dressed in the formal dark suit she had seen so many times. In the manner of Donald Trump, though he would have hated such a comparison, he wore a bright red tie, a contrast to the perfectly ironed white shirt that gave him something of a superior, pugnacious air.

On the desk in front of him lay a newspaper; Oscar's newspaper open at the double page spread. She saw again the headline in its eye catching heavy print. This was the moment of her high noon, the moment her career might end she knew. Finally he looked up.

Dawkins spoke calmly at first. "Maggie have you seen this?" he asked.

He turned the paper towards her.

"Yes Sir Stephen, I have," she replied. The statement was true enough. Her voice betrayed no hint of nerves for right at this moment Maggie was filled with moral courage that affirmed to her she had no reason for regret.

For a moment there was silence in the room.

"This is an article that is explosive," declared Sir Stephen. "It contains a number of revelations about our efforts to negotiate with the EU. Downing Street have been on the line furious, not least because it appears to be written from an inside source."

He held his breath pausing to test her reaction. She said nothing.

Dawkins now leant forward and continued: "The strange thing is that the article appears to highlight many of the points you raised in your report to me."

Maggie was not to be intimidated. Her mind flashed to her heroes Churchill and Alfred; how they would have shown not a hint of fright as they confronted their adversaries. Her response was assertive but polite.

"Points Sir Stephen that were extremely valid and which you redacted from the report!" She looked him in the eye unafraid by the position in which she was putting herself. Attack would be the best form of defence. Besides she now had nothing to lose she surmised.

"Points which run against our loyalty to Downing Street," he instantly retaliated, glowering at her. Now his voice gave vent to his anger. But Maggie undeterred interrupted his flow.

"To whom should our loyalty be Sir Stephen? Tell me that. To Downing Street or to the people, for clearly they are not the same thing?"

She leant across the table and fixed him with her stare. "Let me tell you something sir. 17.4 million people and 85% of voters at the General Election voted to come out of the customs union and the single market. It was made crystal clear. In other words for us no longer to have to adhere to laws made and enforced by unelected overseas bureaucrats. It is those people sir that require our loyalty and anything else is a denial of democracy."

For a brief moment in time Sir Stephen Dawkins was flummoxed and not for the first time from this impudent woman. His face suddenly grew red around the temples as he exploded.

"Our loyalty is to the Prime Minister, to Downing Street!" he thundered. "I am presuming it was you who wrote this article?" He picked up the newspaper and shook it at her.

"I did indeed sir. It is probably the most virtuous thing I have ever done," she replied with immaculate composure. Sir Stephen Dawkins slammed the paper on to the desk.

"Hang your moral scruples you fucking little shit. What the hell shall I tell Downing Street? You're suspended. Get out of my office!"

Maggie rose from her chair shocked by his outburst but strangely calm and self assured. As she walked through the door she turned and answered his question.

"Try Churchill sir. Thou art weighed in the balance and been found wanting."

Chapter 18

Maggie sat quite still in her office, her door closed firmly shut. She took her phone off the hook and turned off her mobile knowing that she needed no interruptions, just silence, immersed in her own thoughts as the momentous events of recent days sank in. Somehow with great character and fortitude she had not allowed Dawkins' fury to move her to tears. Moreover, whilst she had been assertive she had unlike him, remained calm and polite throughout. In effect she knew she may have ruined her career but she had won the argument and done so with dignity.

However, the depression she had felt in the cathedral at Brussels had not lifted. She had been a part of something that appalled her. There was no denying it. Long after her colleagues in their prestigious Whitehall offices had gone home she sat silently contemplating her situation. She had stood her ground; she had constructively and courteously fought the great battle, she had done her duty.

But she had failed the people she represented. She could have resigned months ago. But instead she had remained in her job and allowed herself to be an accessory to the bungling and capricious behaviour that had broken every law of negotiation and insulted her integrity. Others could live with their consciences but Maggie was not at all certain she

214

could live with hers. The standards to which she had tried to live her life had been perhaps irretrievably, cast asunder.

However it wasn't just Dawkins that she blamed. The real blame she knew lay with Downing Street – Downing Street and the Cabinet. Not only the Remainers but those Brexiteer Ministers who unlike their principled colleagues who resigned in disgust, had remained in support of the Prime Minister allowing the great deceit to continue. These were the lackeys; the hypocritical lackeys who had espoused the noble Brexit cause but when the going had got tough had melted like snowflakes as the latest bout of outrageous propaganda had poured forth from the Bank of England. In collusion with the Treasury the nightmare scenarios had reached new, even more preposterous levels calculated to leave grown men in convulsions of despair, unable to sleep and contemplating suicide with only one way in which to save themselves – which was to support and save the Prime Minister.

The last time she had visited the Globe flashed through Maggie's mind when she had watched intently as Henry V had addressed his troops on the eve of Agincourt. These pathetic Brexiteers, these pitiful Cabinet lackeys, these men of straw were to Maggie surely the reincarnated souls of those who Shakespeare described as those who should 'hold their manhoods cheap and think themselves accursed' they had failed in their patriotic duty. These were not 'the few, the happy few, the band of brothers' who had gallantly stiffened their sinews and risen to the call. No, these were the unworthy lackeys who when their children asked of them 'What did you do daddy at Britain's fateful hour?' would hold their heads in their hands as they drowned in shame.

215

Indeed Maggie perused, these were surely the very sons – and daughters – of those who had made parley with the Vikings, settled for the quiet life and put their hands to their ears when Alfred had called them to rally to the fight.

For whatever reason, suddenly Maggie felt her swirling mind beginning to calm. She ran her hands through her hair as if hoping instinctively the act would somehow raise her spirits. She looked at her watch. It was nearly 6.00 yet she felt in no rush to leave. As she sat deep in thought, she slowly became aware her silence was being broken. Outside the noise of people could be discerned. It was strange and somehow disconcerting. She had never heard it before. Nevertheless she chose to ignore it. Then, before she left her office for what would probably be the last time, she checked her laptop for the latest news.

She was shocked at what she read. The angry marchers had reached the centre of London and as dusk had descended thousands of them were beginning to enter Parliament Square. The situation was turning ugly just as she had predicted. She stood up and gazed out of the window. The noise of loudhailers just a street or two away could be clearly heard now. A hundred yards away at the junction to Whitehall she could make out streams of people some carrying banners, striding towards Parliament. For a moment she wondered whether she could make it back to Kensington.

Undaunted she stood up and prepared herself to leave. She paused just for a second taking a cursory glance in the mirror her predecessor had left hanging by the door. Checking her appearance was not something Maggie did often. But for some reason unknown to her, now was such an occasion when she felt the need. She did not look her best she knew as she registered the look of stress that was etched upon her pretty face. Nevertheless she put her shoulders back and forced herself to stand chin up and upright. She walked out of her office, closing the door firmly behind her. She did not look back. Neither would she join the noisy throng no matter how tempting it might be. She may have been suspended but she was also a civil servant, the servant of these people, standing above the fray. She would behave accordingly even now.

Outside, the scene that met Maggie's eyes filled her with fear. She had never found herself in such a situation before and it worried her. Across Whitehall up to Trafalgar Square, along the Mall and beyond, an angry sea of people was striding forward. Thousands now had pressed into Parliament Square as the early evening had taken hold. Near Big Ben police were trying in vain to hold back the pressing crowds marching in close tight lines across Westminster Bridge. A deafening noise filled the air. "BETRAYAL" they were chanting, "BETRAYAL."

Trying hard to stay close to the walls of the buildings she moved slowly but inexorably on. For just an instant her mind flashed to Alfred's wife Ellie as she herself had stood outside the fray. But now she felt herself being half carried by the melee; a twig at the mercy of a stream in full flood. Now the mayhem was all around her, every marcher seemingly carrying banners and loudhailers, pressing forward; a great multitude of angry people striding on. Ahead she could make out the lines of riot police with shields and batons and automatic weapons overtly on display.

She looked back up towards Trafalgar Square straining her eyes to take in the scene. Nelson would have seen them far below she mused. Now on this day close to the anniversary of Trafalgar, what would he be saying to them she wondered? She knew the answer: 'England expects every man to do his duty' she thought. How apt Nelson's famous order seemed as she watched her countrymen rousing themselves demanding the freedom Nelson had secured.

And there above the fray stood proud the singular dignity of the Cenotaph; an iconic and indeed ironic quiet symbol respected and applauded by the marchers forging by. Didn't it represent the very essence of their fight for nationhood, for freedom, for the sacrifice that sovereignty demanded?

As Maggie took in the scene she felt herself being stirred, sensing the anger and empathetic to the passions all around her. This was like a movie scene she imagined; an epic movie with thousands of extras that told of a profound and noble story. Her hero Alfred shot through her mind. She imagined his own freedom fighters advancing up the shallow gradient at Bratton Camp. Like the people here they too were armed with almost nothing as they faced the phalanx of the Viking line, their shields interlocked determined to hold their ground. The police here too had their shields tightly drawn, raised against missiles thrown just as the Vikings had as they resisted Alfred's onslaught.

In the centre of the marchers the most well known Brexiteers sat upon the shoulders of their followers. Like Alfred they were protected by their loyal lieutenants as they gestured, exhorting their followers on. Maggie looked up spotting the helicopters overhead. Their lights were haphazardly and intimidatingly circling the melee below. Then as the din reached another crescendo she felt herself suddenly pushed forward in the scrum. It was then she saw the water cannon; she saw too the army trucks depositing soldiers quickly taking up positions, standing abreast at Churchill's statue. The irony struck her instantly as she pictured the great man fighting for the people's freedom just as Alfred had.

Behind the front ranks more lines of marchers were advancing now from every direction, pushing forward in tight lines just as at Edington rallying to the cause; onward ever onward to regain the bastion of liberty that lay ahead. And as she watched the police lines in riot gear withstanding the onslaught outside Parliament, she felt her mind again swirling; out of control; ignited now by a cocktail of adrenaline and stimulation.

She pictured Cromwell; how he had taken soldiers inside and saved Parliament from the disreputable insult to the people it had become. How apt she thought, how very apt. Parliament both before the referendum and after had promised the vote would be binding. Yet ever since this sorry spectacle, this mother of Parliaments once so respected, had once again become the beacon that far from representing the people's wishes, had dignified itself only by stupefying arrogance drowning itself in its own self importance; an insult to democracy and the facilitator to the greatest national humiliation since Suez; a travesty of its former glory. But perhaps, just perhaps she wondered, this Parliament would come to its senses and throw out the capitulation agreement and its principal, though not principled, protagonist in Downing Street, just as eighty years previously it had forced out the previous occupier by the name of Chamberlain.

But what would they put in its place? Many dishonourable members instead of getting behind the British negotiators, were using every mechanism to thwart the democratic will. Despite the referendum being binding this motley group who for years had been happy to pass powers to Brussels might now use Parliament to demand a second vote in order to sign away their country's sovereignty. Their self-righteous hypocrisy was breathtaking; an abrogation of responsibility on a vast and unprecedented scale. Indeed in former times such treachery would surely have seen these traitorous misfits thrown into the Tower!

By now the darkness was descending. Torches had been lit by the thousands of protesters now tightly packed across Parliament Square and beyond. Bonfires too were being set alight, all the while police helicopters circling menacingly overhead, their spotlights tensely monitoring the mayhem below. Now Maggie felt herself moving almost uncontrollably, forced on by the heaving mass of people; now being thrown in this direction then that by the jostling angry crowd like a pebble on the beach at the mercy of a pounding sea.

But this was a sea of human flesh, angry and resolute people determined to be heard. To call them a mob would have been an insult. For these were the antithesis of the angry brigade; these were the angry silent majority. In other circumstances the phrase would have seemed an oxymoron of sorts but now it was real; the innocent law abiding citizens who had naively put their trust in their Government believing their vote would be respected now roused in indignation. These were the principled decent people of middle England who had put down their Daily Telegraphs and got up from their sofas to make their stand.

But there too united with them in common cause were

the solid working classes, the unpretentious salt of the earth types that cared not a jot for the values of the metropolitan elite, but for the cornerstones of nationhood their fathers had sacrificed for, namely the simple, the sublime aspiration of sovereignty: the natural right to liberty enshrined by their cousins across the pond in the American Declaration of Independence and Constitution; indeed as fought for by Alfred's followers – the simple patriotic right to make their own laws in their own land.

But politicians believing they knew best had seen to that. Now aroused and furious, the people would no longer be mocked and humiliated. Their voices would be heard. All around the chanting was now reaching a fresh intensity. "WE WANT SOVEREIGNTY" they bayed. "WHAT DO WE WANT? OUR LAWS, OUR BORDERS, OUR MONEY" they chanted.

Maggie suddenly swung around taken like a feather in the maelstrom pushed and shoved by the force of the crush. Now she found herself staring at the famous faces that had kept the torch of freedom alive and led the movement for Brexit against the odds that had frightened the establishment to the very core. These men and women deserved medals like former heroes she thought.

Yes they had been mocked by that unattractive element of Remainers who had defied the people's will using every ruse, backed up by foreign funds and driven by an insufferable smugness that they knew best. Yet others who had voted Remain like Maggie's dear friend Stella, were decent good hearted folk, principled democrats who had respected the majority vote and had wished only that the Government had got on with it.

Suddenly Maggie's attention was diverted. An effigy defaced and unrecognizable was burning fiercely, its flames shooting high above the square piercing the early night sky. The helicopters veered quickly fearing their fuel tanks would be ignited and turned into a raging fireball, an inferno that could fall upon the crowd at any moment. Now their din and the noise of sirens, the incessant police loudhailers, the chanting of the protesters came together producing an ear splitting cacophony of sound. And all around the crowds were surging in a cauldron of energy being pushed from behind and from every which way; a people's revolution in the making.

Yet slowly and with the greatest effort Maggie had continued to force her way around the edge of the mayhem. As she moved toward Victoria she looked around again in disbelief. A mother and young child had been crushed in the stampede. She tried to help. Sirens were wailing but police cars and ambulances had halted unable to get through the protesters ahead. Only eventually the crowds thinned like dark clouds allowing occasional rays of sunshine suggestive of hope to come.

Onward she struggled, staring at the boarded up shops wondering how this could be happening in dear old England, the home to the mother of Parliaments. As she walked she took in the angry faces, a mixture of resolve and opprobrium written upon them – so different from the faces of jubilation of Alfred's victorious freedom fighters she imagined.

Eventually she made it to Victoria station only to find all the tubes had been stopped: central London had been brought now to an undignified halt. Like Alfred's stalwart followers she would have to walk and walk she did. Five hours had passed since her denouement with Dawkins by the time she reached the quiet respite of Kensington Church Street.

Safe inside Maggie Taylor stood under the shower for a long time. She took the water as cool as she could bear, somehow deep inside wanting to cleanse herself of all that she had been through.

That night as she slept she dreamt of that last visit to her parents. The lunch overlooking Poole Harbour, the hugs her mother had given and most of all, the words of pride in her expressed by her father. But the shame she felt had not been miraculously eviscerated, wiped clean and erased as if the last few awful months had been nothing but a dream. Thus when the early light of dawn indicated another day she pulled the duvet higher and shut her eyes again. But as morning came the magical power of silence was broken. She reached over in her half sleep and picked up the phone. She listened as Crispin Urquart spoke in a tense sombre voice.

"Is that you Maggie? This is Crispin. I can't hear you very well, are you all right?" He paused.

"I have heard about what happened to you. I am so very sorry. Let's meet and talk. You are not alone, you know."

"Thank you Crispin, I appreciate that," she said. Her voice came slowly.

"Maggie, turn on the news. The Brexiteers are laying siege to Downing Street. Apparently 15,000 are at the main gates and another 7,000 at Horseguards. The police are pinned against the railings. They are armed Maggie, armed as you know. The place could ignite at any moment. Anything could happen now." Crispin sounded tense and agitated in equal measure.

She rose from the bed and as she did so she noticed her reflection in the mirror. Her face was drawn; a harrowed look had replaced her prettiness. She pushed her hair back off her face but it made little difference. She slipped on a towel dressing gown and pulled it tightly around her as if a source of protection to the sudden feelings of vulnerability that overwhelmed her. She turned on the television. Sure enough live pictures were coming through of the mayhem he had described.

She dropped the phone as she watched in horror. Police were pointing their automatic weapons above the people's heads. The offices on either side of Downing Street had been entered and occupied. Now the people had reached the upper levels just as Alfred had done at Edington. Hundreds of eggs were being rained down upon the police. Eggs against automatic weapons, it was absurd. Maggie thought instantly of the Anglo-Saxons armed with little more, clashing against the well armed Viking Army of Guthrum. She thought of Alfred's ever tightening siege at Chippenham as she stared in disbelief.

Her faced etched with shock, she stood mesmerised watching as cameras aboard helicopters overhead showed angry people surging forward, blood streaming down their faces as they faced the bruising batons. The announcer called them protesters: freedom fighters would have been a more accurate term. One thing she knew, they were not rioters in any sense of the word. These were ordinary people driven on by a toxic mixture of pent up anger and frustration, their only motive being their democratic rights to be observed.

Could this really be Britain she wondered. This was not the home of some power hungry despot determined to cling on to power and live with the accusation of treachery, surely? This was Britain, Great Britain, the country which took the people's rights seriously and respected them. She switched the television off unable to bring herself to watch anymore. It was all so shocking; it was all so depressing. Above all Maggie knew – it was all so avoidable.

She stood lonely at her window and stared at nothing.

* * *

The young man watched avidly the athletic figure in the pool. The bikini clad woman could have been an Olympic swimmer for all he knew such was the effortless elegance of her crawl as she scythed through the water. His eyes followed her as she completed another length. She stepped out and nonchalantly threw a towel around her shoulders masking her body from any admirers.

It had been the first time Stella had swum since her visit to the Dordogne with Maggie and she had determined now to get back to her regime. The exercise did her good and besides it kept her in good shape she knew. As she walked to the changing room something distracted her. A television on the wall had begun flashing BREAKING NEWS. She paused and looked up and listened to the announcer...

'Huge Remainer marches have now clashed with the Brexiteers in Whitehall. Many are wielding banners demanding a second referendum amidst deafening roars as the crowds surge forward. Some appear intent upon a confrontation, urged on it seems by some celebrity supporters. Ugly clashes are taking place. A number of the Brexiteers have been hurt. Women and even children are lying bleeding on the streets. Ambulances are however unable to reach them. At the same time our reporter close to the Cenotaph confirms the siege of Downing Street is continuing into another day. Nasty clashes have broken out in several major towns and cities up and down the country. The army is on standby. Schools are closed and the government are urging people to stay at home until advised otherwise...'

Stella hurried on. She dressed and began her walk back along the Fulham Road. Three days had passed since the first of the marching columns had entered central London. At least Chelsea had remained as yet unaffected and she felt safe enough as she walked the half mile back to Cadogan Place.

The news of the Remainer clashes did not surprise her. She herself had been a Remainer and many of her friends were principled Remainers who had exercised their democratic rights and then respected the verdict of the majority. But these protesters were of a different ilk. Many had steadfastly refused to accept the democratic wishes not only of the referendum but of the 85% at the General Election who had voted for the two main parties whose manifestos had confirmed departure: even two votes would not be accepted.

The Remainer pressure groups had been led by establishment figures – including a number of MPs – and financed by a foreign billionaire, amongst others: they had been active, running a campaign of subterfuge calculated to upturn Parliament's unequivocal promise that the biggest vote in history would be binding. It had been reported that a knighted Liberal Democrat and assorted Remainer figures had only recently gone to Brussels telling them a second referendum would likely come, in effect giving succour to Britain's negotiating adversaries. After all in three other

European countries when the vote had failed to go the way the EU wished, they had been forced to vote again until they got it right. Britain could surely be forced to do likewise they were certain.

Stella Lawton was not a civil servant but a business woman. To her their tactics were the equivalent of an insider telling a prospective customer how desperate their company was for their business and how they would pay any price, while simultaneously their Sales Director tried in vain to negotiate the most profitable deal. Over the two and a half years since the referendum, they had done inestimable harm in her view, in undermining Britain's negotiating hand at every turn. As Maggie had remarked, these were today's equivalent of Alfred's fifth column who had colluded with their Viking masters.

She objected too that her company, along with the 94% of British companies who sold nothing into Europe, would have to continue to abide by EU laws largely designed to protect German manufacturers. It had been reported Dyson amongst others were taking their manufacturing facilities to the Far East. Yet because of Chequers, exporting their products back to Britain would incur a tariff, not to mention legal requirements set by the EU. So much for taking back control of our laws!

Nevertheless as Stella walked back that day to Cadogan Place she managed to put Brexit out of her mind despite the growing protests now so close at hand.

It was three days later that she received a text from Maggie inviting her to go over that evening. It had mentioned nothing of her suspension from her work or her travails in Brussels and Stella was eager to catch up upon her news.

Excited at the prospect, she had bought a bottle of Bergerac wine for the occasion. It was befitting she thought after their holiday a little while ago. Before she left her flat she paused and glanced at the newspaper that had lain unread since the previous day. After the tumultuous events of the last few days nothing could surprise her now she thought. However, as she took in the front page she sat down without taking her eyes off the paper. It made for grim reading.

Whilst the siege of Downing Street had continued now into a seventh day, it was being rumoured that the Prime Minister instead of stepping down as many had demanded, was about to call a General Election. Yet the opinion polls had put Labour into a twenty point lead as whole swathes of the Conservative faithful had registered their disgust. In response the stock market had slumped. It had already fallen 10% into correction territory: yesterday as the reports circulated, panic had stepped in. The FTSE had plummeted another 4% during the day and if the opinion polls were to be believed, was predicted to fall by as much as a third if the election went to Labour. The impact on pensions, on enterprise and on the economy was almost incalculable.

To her sagacious mind and her understanding of business she was well aware of what the consequences of a hard left government would be. Indeed she had read a report in the financial press just days ago. She could recall the highlights: an instant slump in inward investment; capital flight and the anticipation of the pound reaching parity with the euro within three months and the dollar within two years; mortgage rates tripling as the Bank of England struggled to protect the pound, hold the lid on inflation and offset the enormous rise in government borrowing; a sustained rise in unemployment; companies becoming strangled under government interference and regulation; Britain becoming significantly less competitive; younger generations becoming crippled with mountainous national debt and massive tax rises...the list ran on.

It was the younger generation she knew that had no knowledge of the economic mismanagement of some previous Labour governments and this time, under an economically illiterate neo Marxist regime the report had predicted it would be many times worse. Added to that the Americans were rumoured to stop sharing vital intelligence with Britain, suspicious of where the new government's loyalty lay. In effect Britain would become near defenceless and unable to resist any aggression from any quarter. The consequences of Downing Street's bungled Brexit were becoming shocking in the extreme.

However, it was Labour's eschewing of its election manifesto commitment to take Britain out of the EU's regulatory framework that had really annoyed her. Political expediency had trounced any hint of principle in upholding the referendum result. How different today's Labour Party were to the principled and patriotic party who had lent their support to Churchill in 1940, she thought.

But there was no time now to read the paper in depth. She looked at her watch. It was time to go and as she stepped outside into the bright sunshine amidst a cloudless sky she felt her spirits lift. She took a deep breath of cool autumn air. It felt good to be alive.

Across the road she paused as she noticed the subtle change of colours that had almost surreptitiously taken place in Cadogan Gardens. The grass had received its final cut before winter set in and the beds had retained a well attended look. Several people were sauntering along a meandering path causing the eye to look left and right in admiration. A dog had paused to do its business while its owner walked deftly on pretending not to notice. She would not linger however. She increased her pace toward Sloane Square. At least the tubes had restarted after the last week of travel chaos.

She had made certain to wear her poppy. For today was 11th November 2018 marking 100 years since the end of the Great War. With her knowledge of history Stella was only too aware of the sacrifice that had been made by her countrymen, who along with their colonial friends and allies had secured their freedom and indeed the liberation of Europe also. How ironic she thought that today barely two miles away the issue of freedom was once again being contested.

When she alighted from the tube she walked briskly up Kensington Church Street carrying her Bergerac wine. A hoarding advertising holidays in France caught her eye and memories of their happy time in the Dordogne came flooding back: their fine dining at Monpazier; how they had walked the medieval alleys at Sarlat – and then of course their intimate conversations in which Maggie had talked of the Brexit negotiations and shared her deep concerns. It had only been months before but somehow it seemed longer.

She walked up the steps and entered through the open door. Maggie had put on one of her beloved CDs. She smiled as she recognised the music wafting down the stairs. Nimrod was one of her favourites: how appropriate to be playing Elgar she thought upon this day of remembrance marking the sacrifice for freedom.

"Maggie," she called. "I'm coming up. Have two glasses at the ready, I've got some wine you'll like."

She didn't bother to knock and with a smile upon her face walked into the flat. Then in an instant she heard herself scream uncontrollably as she took in the awful scene, her heart pounding; her brain unable to fathom what she was seeing. Maggie Taylor lay across the sofa.

"Maggie," she yelled, "Maggie!"

For a moment she was frozen to the spot staring at the awful spectacle. Maggie's body was shockingly still as she had never seen before, her head back a look of sadness etched upon her pretty face. Yet perhaps just perhaps, her initial instincts were false; merely mendacious rumours playing in her mind.

Without knowing what she was doing, driven only by her instincts, she began to shake her friend as if to wake her. For a moment in time she felt phased, out of control and unable to think clearly, beholden to whatever fate had determined – perhaps but a terrible dream, her imagination playing with her in some perverted way, her eyes deluding her. She shook dear Maggie again but her eyes were closed and her limbs seemed lifeless. She grasped her wrist and tried to feel for a pulse. Now, with her brain beginning to take back control in the frantic battle with her emotions, Stella dialled 999.

"Ambulance please. Please come quickly," she cried as she gave the details. Again she felt herself freeze. She listened for a moment. The Elgar CD was still playing. Nimrod's majestic repetitive melody had reached its climax, the glorious sound broken only by her sobbing. Still she couldn't believe what she was taking in: this terrible sight, poor Maggie; this lovely person; this epitome of integrity; this beautiful friend she had known lying in her arms. If only her tears pouring down her cheeks could wash away the sight. But these were tears uncontrollably confirming that what she was seeing appeared real, undeniable; confirming and forcing her to accept the unthinkable; that this was Maggie, her dear friend Maggie Taylor, a person she had liked and respected beyond measure. She clung to her as if in some unfathomable way she could at least let her know in death that she was loved. For a minute or more she gripped her head in her arms crying uncontrollably and screamed out her name.

And then she saw on the coffee table the empty bottle. Perhaps, she imagined the hospital could empty her stomach of its contents. But surely, surely she was deluding herself and it was too late. Beside it lay four white envelopes. Stella looked at each in turn. One was addressed to 'Dear Mum and Dad xxx'. Another to 'Oscar', still another to the 'Prime Minister'. And then underneath was one with her own name scrawled upon it. She tore it open and as her tears fell upon the paper she forced her eyes to focus and cried aloud Maggie's words...

My dear Stella

I am so so sorry for you to have read this. Please try to understand because you don't know how bad it has been. I have been a party Stella to terrible incompetence but also humiliation to the people we represent which is perhaps even worse. Please understand. Please also pass the letter I have left to my parents who I know will be heartbroken. There is also a letter revealing more of our cringing negotiation to Oscar. I feel so strongly Stella the truth must out. For what it is worth please also ensure my letter to the Prime Minister reaches No.10.

I hope you can try to understand Stella. I am just so incredibly depressed. After our wonderful time together in the Dordogne we discussed how similar the deception today has been to Munich. Yet I can tell you this is far worse, because it has not just been naivety but a deliberate reneging of promises to respect the will of the people – promises that proved simply disingenuous, aided and abetted by various Parliamentarians. I have been a party to treachery; to the betrayal of the 85% at the 2017 General Election who voted no longer to be rule takers, and the 17.4 million at the referendum Stella. We may now indeed become a country of rule takers – a vassal state in effect and I simply cannot live with the guilt I feel.

If my life, if my tiny microcosm of contribution in the scheme of things is to have any meaning, any purpose or legacy then I need at the day of judgement to have redeemed myself and given it value. Too many people have discarded their moral integrity and sabotaged a free global Britain Stella, but I will not be one of them. I am no longer able to live this life knowing that I have participated in this monstrous betrayal.

I am so sorry to have caused you, my friends and most of all my family such hurt, but I have no choice…please, please understand Stella.

With love for the rest of your life

Maggie xx

UNRESOLVED –The Sequel …to follow.

Also by Philip St Lawrence:
Message from Joshua – Part One
Message from Joshua – Part Two

As a professional speaker he gives talks to Historical
Societies & others upon
ALFRED THE GREAT – his DARKEST HOUR
For information please contact
greatesthour@outlook.com
The author also gives corporate presentations upon topics
including negotiation skills & leadership.